Shamrock Shenanigans

By

Kathi Daley

This book is a work of fiction. Names, characters, places, and incidents either are products of the author's imagination or are used fictitiously. Any resemblance to actual events or locales or persons, living or dead, is entirely coincidental.

This book is dedicated to my son Danny, who currently lives in Dublin and is attending Trinity College.

I also want to thank the very talented Jessica Fischer for the cover art.

I so appreciate Bruce Curran, who is always ready and willing to answer my cyber questions.

And, of course, thanks to the readers and bloggers in my life, who make doing what I do possible.

Thank you to Randy Ladenheim-Gil for the editing.

Special thanks to Nancy Farris, Pamela Curran, Vivian Shane, Della Williamson, Teri Fish, and Janel Flynn for submitting recipes.

And finally I want to thank my sister Christy for always lending an ear and my husband Ken for allowing me time to write by taking care of everything else.

Books by Kathi Daley

Come for the murder, stay for the romance.

Zoe Donovan Cozy Mystery:

Halloween Hijinks
The Trouble With Turkeys
Christmas Crazy
Cupid's Curse
Big Bunny Bump-off
Beach Blanket Barbie
Maui Madness
Derby Divas
Haunted Hamlet
Turkeys, Tuxes, and Tabbies
Christmas Cozy
Alaskan Alliance
Matrimony Meltdown
Soul Surrender
Heavenly Honeymoon
Hopscotch Homicide
Ghostly Graveyard
Santa Sleuth
Shamrock Shenanigans

Zimmerman Academy Shorts

The New Normal – *January 2016*

Paradise Lake Cozy Mystery:

Pumpkins in Paradise
Snowmen in Paradise
Bikinis in Paradise
Christmas in Paradise
Puppies in Paradise
Halloween in Paradise

Whales and Tails Cozy Mystery:

Romeow and Juliet
The Mad Catter
Grimm's Furry Tail
Much Ado About Felines
Legend of Tabby Hollow
Cat of Christmas Past
A Tale of Two Tabbies – *February 2016*

Seacliff High Mystery:

The Secret
The Curse
The Relic
The Conspiracy
The Grudge

Road to Christmas Romance:
Road to Christmas Past

The Cast

The Contestants and their guests:
Zoe Donovan – amateur sleuth
Zak Zimmerman – Zoe's husband and plus one
Jessica Fielding – mystery writer
Cassandra Fielding – Jessica's niece and plus one
Sam Spalding – private detective
Susan Langtree – Sam's assistant and plus one
Millie Monroe – psychic who has helped authorities solve crimes
Piper Belmont – Millie's plus one
Armand Waller – history professor and relic hunter
Luke Sutton – Waller's teaching assistant and plus one

Also attending:
Brent Silverwood – actor doing character study
Drew Baltimore – reporter covering event

The Host and Staff:
Lord Fergus Dunphy – host
Bonnie – cook
Liza – maid
Liam – stable hand
Byron – server/bartender

Resident Ghosts:

Catherine Dunphy – was married to Carrick Dunphy in the mid- to late-1600s

Meghan Dunphy – was married to Aiden Dunphy in the 1800s

Birte Dunphy – was married to the lord in the mid-1700s

Rowena Dunphy – Lord Dunphy's mother, who passed away ten years ago

Finnian Newton– Rowena's brother, who passed away six years ago

Chapter 1

Thursday, February 11

There were twelve of us sitting at the table waiting for our host, Lord Dunphy, to arrive. I can't tell you how excited I was to be spending Valentine's Day at a real Irish castle. Talk about a dream come true. And the best part: the castle was purported to be haunted by not one but several distinct ghosts.

"This is so exciting," I said to Piper Belmont, the woman behind my invitation to this very special murder mystery event. "I wonder if we'll see any ghosts this weekend."

"When Poppy and I were here last I'm certain we were visited by Birte Dunphy. She was married to the lord back in the mid-seventeen hundreds. They say she really ran things and the old lord was merely a pawn. According to some, she is still in charge, imposing her will from beyond the grave."

"You think she's controlling the new lord in some way?"

"It would seem that she might be," Piper answered. "The man is a bit loopy at times. Poppy doesn't really care for his tendency to blunder his way through life, but I think he is just trying to run things in the twenty-first century while attempting to keep Birte happy at the same time."

"I can see how that might be difficult."

"Especially when you throw Rowena into the mix."

"Rowena?" I asked.

"Lord Dunphy's overbearing mother. She passed on about ten years ago and has been haunting him ever since. It you ask me, the struggle between Birte and Rowena to control the goings-on in the castle has driven poor Fergus insane. Literally."

"Fergus is the first name of the current Lord Dunphy?" I clarified.

"Yes, dear."

"Are all the ghosts female?"

"Not at all. Fergus's Uncle Finnian has been known to make an appearance from time to time. He died five, no, maybe six years ago. In life he was browbeaten by his sister Rowena. He never married or did much of anything. After Rowena passed he attempted to sow his wild oats, but he really didn't know how to manage himself without his sister manipulating his every move. He drank himself to death in just a few years. I personally have not had the opportunity to be haunted by the man, but I hear he's a hoot."

"So if the current lord's mother and uncle are still haunting the place is his father here as well?"

"Dear lord no. The man couldn't wait to die to make his escape. I'm pretty sure he headed toward the distant light before his body was even cold."

I tried to sort things out as Piper turned to speak to the woman sitting next to her. Zak and I had met Piper and her husband Charles (Poppy) while we were honeymooning on Heavenly Island. We'd invited them to lunch so Zak and I could interrogate them about the death of another visitor to the island who, at the time, I had been suspected of killing. During the course of that lunch we'd established their innocence and moved on to talk of the world-traveling couple's recent escapades. Charles and Piper had visited a haunted castle—a different one— – and I had been fascinated by the idea of visiting such a location. When Piper had heard about this murder mystery party, which had been organized as a game to pit five contestants with crime-solving backgrounds against one another, she'd remembered our conversation and scored Zak and me an invite.

Charles hadn't wanted to attend, and neither Piper nor Charles had any sort of mystery-solving tendencies, so Piper had asked Lord Dunphy to invite her psychic, an older woman named Millie Monroe. Each contestant was allowed to bring a guest, so Piper had come along as Millie's plus one. It seemed this eccentric ghost whisperer had helped law enforcement to solve crimes on more than one occasion.

Everyone quieted down when Lord Dunphy entered the room. He took his seat at the head of the table. He looked at each person in turn, snarling at some and winking at others, before he began to speak. "Welcome. What a fascinating lot. It's not often there are so many conflicting auras in the room. This should be interesting."

Everyone sat silently while the lord pulled a flask from his jacket pocket and took a swig of something I assumed was alcohol-based. I glanced at Zak. He shrugged. What did the man mean by conflicting auras? He really was a bit of a kook.

"First of all I must inform you all that the rain has caused the river to breech its banks and flood the bridge. I am afraid we are quite isolated on Dunphy Island until the water recedes. But not to worry; this happens quite often and we have plenty of food and drink for your enjoyment."

A huge clap of thunder vibrated through the old stone walls of the castle, as if on cue. I noticed that several of the guests began to whisper among themselves. I guess there was an extraspooky factor when you considered that we were not only staying in a haunted castle but were trapped with a loony host and a handful of ghosts.

"Before we serve the meal, I'd like to introduce everyone," Lord Dunphy continued.

The man looked directly at me.

"To my right is Zoe Donovan, amateur sleuth, from Ashton Falls, in the United States. She is accompanied by her husband, Zak Zimmerman, and her little dog Charlie, who, I assume, is waiting for you in your room?"

"Yes, he's in the room," I verified.

"And the room is to your liking?"

"Yes, it's lovely. I understand it used to be Catherine Dunphy's room when she was alive."

"Yes, that is correct," Lord Dunphy confirmed. "Catherine was married to Carrick Dunphy in the mid- to late-sixteen hundreds. Unlike many of the Dunphy brides, who were brought to the castle in arranged marriages, Catherine loved her husband very much. She bore him twelve children, all sons."

Yikes.

"It is said that Carrick gifted Catherine with a precious gem on the birth of each son. History tells us that Carrick obtained only the most valuable gems, and legend tells us that the gems are still hidden somewhere in the castle," Lord Dunphy continued. "While I would like to think that was true, I've not been able to find any of them, and believe me, I've looked."

"How did Catherine die?" I asked.

"She contracted a fever not long after the birth of her twelfth son. I imagine an infection of some sort developed. She died in the room in which you are staying, surrounded by her husband and surviving children. By all reports her passing was peaceful. I'm not certain why she did not pass on at the time of her death, although there are those who say she couldn't bear to leave the man she loved so very much."

"That's so sad. Did Carrick remarry?"

"He did not. He went to his death honoring the woman he considered to be the love of a lifetime."

I thought I might cry. How sad and romantic. "Is Carrick still haunting the castle as well?"

"Not as far as I know."

"I'm surprised Catherine didn't move on once Carrick passed," I commented.

"I can't claim to know Catherine's motivation for staying, but she does appear to still be about. She tends to become more active when there are guests in the castle, especially when there are people staying in her room. I think there is a very good chance you will receive a visit from her during your stay."

Awesome.

Lord Dunphy turned his attention back to the table as a whole. "To Mr. Zimmerman's right is Jessica Fielding, and her niece and guest Cassandra Fielding. Jessica is a *New York Times* best-selling mystery writer who likes to take a stab at solving cold cases in her spare time."

Jessica was an older woman, a little on the plump side, with a friendly face, which, in my opinion, provided a stark contrast to the eagle-sharp look of her eyes. She smiled and chatted with those around her, but it seemed obvious to me that she was sizing everyone up and making judgments as she worked her way around the table.

Her niece, Cassandra, was probably around my age, late twenties, with a friendly smile that seemed to be genuine and an easygoing way about her. She had thick dark hair pulled back with a clip, and a smattering of freckles across her nose, giving her the simple look of the girl next door. I hadn't as of yet had a chance to speak to her, but of everyone in attendance she appeared to be the most approachable.

"Does the room I am staying in belong to a ghost?" Jessica asked.

"As a matter of fact, the room you are in belonged to Meghan O'Brian Dunphy. Meghan came to the castle as the young bride of Aiden Dunphy, the eldest son of the lord of the castle in the early eighteen hundreds. I'm afraid Aiden and Meghan did not enjoy a marriage based on love, as Carrick and Catherine did. Less than a month after she arrived at the castle she was found dead on the stone walkway below her bedroom window. Some say she was so unhappy in her role as wife to a man she detested that she jumped, while others claim her new husband grew tired of her and pushed her to her death."

"Poor dear," Jessica commented. "Living with a man of your choosing is bad enough, but being forced to spend time with a man you barely know would be unbearable."

I watched as Jessica whispered something to Cassandra, who gave Jessica a knowing glance, barely suppressing a chuckle. I could only imagine that neither woman was a fan of marriage.

"To Ms. Fielding's right we have Sam Spalding and his assistant and guest, Susan Langtree," Lord Dunphy continued. "Sam is an accomplished private detective who works out of San Francisco in the state of California."

Sam was a short, thin man who was dressed so stereotypically that it had to be a ruse. He not only wore the standard fedora and trench coat, which was completely inappropriate for dinner, but he had a huge cigar that he played with but, fortunately, didn't light.

His assistant, Susan, was a good foot taller than he was but also on the thin side. She wore a red evening gown that was as out of place at the dinner table as Sam's hat and trench coat. I didn't know this for certain, but it almost appeared that Sam Spalding had worn the goofy outfit to appear as a less than serious person in an attempt to throw everyone off.

Neither Sam nor Susan asked about a ghost.

Lord Dunphy turned his attention to the opposite side of the table. "Across from Sam and Susan we have Professor Armand Waller and his teaching assistant and guest, Luke Sutton. Professor Waller is a world-renowned scholar, who, in addition to teaching, travels the world tracking down lost artifacts."

Professor Waller looked to be in his late fifties or early sixties. He wore a pair of dress slacks and a corduroy jacket that was very outdated but of good quality. He was of average height and build and wore little round glasses that gave him a constant look of surprise.

His teaching assistant was tall and muscular and looked to be in his early thirties. I couldn't help but notice him noticing Sam's assistant, Susan. She appeared to be giving him flirty glances as well. If I had to guess, there would be more hanky panky than investigating going on between the two of them.

"Sitting next to Mr. Sutton is Brent Silverwood. Brent is not a contestant in the game but rather an actor, here to do a character study for a film that will be set in a castle much like mine. He promises to observe and not get in the way, as does the woman sitting next to him, Drew Baltimore. Drew is a freelance reporter, here to cover the story of our little murder mystery."

If Brent hadn't been introduced as an actor I would still guess him to be one. Tall and fit, with bleached blond hair, a spray-on tan, teeth so white they almost blinded you, and a cocky, killer smile, Brent looked exactly like the type of man Hollywood fantasies were made of.

Likewise, Drew tended to look her part. She was dressed conservatively and wore minimal makeup. Her dark brown hair was neatly pulled away from her face and large glasses gave her a look of intelligence.

"And last but not least," Lord Dunphy concluded, "we have Millie Monroe, a popular psychic, and her guest, the delightful Piper Belmont."

I couldn't help but notice the way Lord Dunphy smiled at Piper. Were the two of them involved in a fling? I would be surprised if Piper was cheating on her husband, who she seemed to adore, but I couldn't deny the way the sophisticated woman was lustily staring at our host. Maybe there was more to this murder mystery weekend than I'd thought.

I looked around the table one more time as Lord Dunphy signaled the server, whose name I had discovered was Byron, to bring the first course. Although there were twelve people present—thirteen if you counted Lord Dunphy—there were only five contestants: myself, Jessica Fielding, Sam Spalding, Armand Waller, and Millie Monroe. It was my guess that none of us, or our guests, would be either the victim or the killer. I had to admit I was excited to get started. I'd solved more than my share of real murders in the past, but a fake murder would be just as much fun without all the angst. Or so I thought.

"So what do you think?" I asked Zak after the group retired to the parlor for drinks and conversation once the five-course meal had been consumed.

"I think it's late and we've had a long day. Would it be rude to excuse ourselves and head up to our room?"

I looked around the gathering place. Byron had taken off the uniform he'd worn to wait on the table and slipped into the bartender role. Everyone appeared to be having a wonderful time. Piper had disappeared shortly after dinner, as had Lord Dunphy, who'd announced that he needed to see to the final arrangements for the game, which would begin the following day. Maybe they *were* having a fling. Charles did travel a lot, and I imagined Piper got bored when he was away. Still, I was surprised that she would be so obvious as to sneak away minutes after Lord Dunphy, if she was heading for a secret rendezvous. Perhaps she was part of the game and had simply gone off to prepare.

"Do you think Piper might be part of the game as either the victim or the killer?" I whispered.

"I suppose she might. She does seem to have a relationship of some sort with his lordship."

"You noticed that too? And she did disappear shortly after Lord Dunphy excused himself."

"True, but she wasn't the only one to excuse herself," Zak pointed out. "Armand claimed to have a headache and went up to his room immediately after dinner and I saw Susan and Luke sneak off a little while ago."

"Based on what I observed when they were introduced, I'm going to guess they headed off for a little hanky panky."

"Hanky panky sounds good," Zak whispered. "I can't wait to make love to my wife in that antique bed. Perhaps we should head upstairs as well."

I couldn't help but think of Catherine's twelve sons and wonder if the room hadn't been cursed with a fertility spell. Not that being able to bear children was a curse. Exactly. But twelve? In the back of my mind I couldn't help but wonder if staying in the room Catherine had shared with the love of *her* lifetime, with the love of *my* lifetime, wouldn't result in a similar outcome.

"Do you think our room is cursed?" I asked Zak.

"Cursed?"

"Never mind." I knew I was being ridiculous. I was sure there had been dozens if not hundreds of people who slept in that room over the past three centuries. I doubted any of them had ended up with twelve sons. "We can go up in a minute. I want to take this opportunity to size everyone up. It seems like there really are five contestants, and each of the five has brought a guest. I doubt any of us is either the victim or the killer and I don't think any of the guests are either. It would be too hard for the guest of one of the contestants to keep from giving their identity away. That just leaves Brent, Drew, or a staff member to play the two roles, unless Piper is in on it, in which case Millie must be in on it as well."

Zak sighed. I could see he wasn't thrilled that I wanted to talk, but I really needed to work this through in my mind before I could relax and enjoy the evening.

I looked around the room. Jessica was speaking to Sam Spalding. Based on their body language it seemed possible they may have been acquainted prior to their arrival at the castle. Jessica's niece Cassandra was chatting with the psychic, Millie Monroe, and the reporter, Drew Baltimore. Neither Armand, Piper, Luke, nor Susan had returned to the group, and Brent had left a short while ago to make a phone call.

"Did you notice that Armand seemed particularly quiet during dinner?" I asked Zak.

"He did claim to have a headache. I suppose that could be the source of his disinclination to participate in the conversation."

"Yeah, I suppose."

"I think it's too early in the game to start looking for clues in the behavior of the others. I think we should get a good night's rest and once the victim is revealed we can take it from there."

"I guess you're right. There doesn't seem to be much that can be learned from this evening's gathering. Besides, we still need to let Charlie out. Perhaps we should make our excuses and head upstairs."

Zak smiled a wicked little grin.

Luckily, both Zak and I thought to bring raincoats and waterproof boots. The introductory letter we'd been sent when we'd signed up for the weekend informed us that the area received a lot of rain on an annual basis. It had been pouring since we'd arrived at the airport, and it seemed to be coming down even harder since we'd arrived at the castle. Part of me wanted to be concerned about the velocity of the storm, but the old stone structure had been standing for centuries and I was sure it had weathered worse.

Charlie was happy to get outdoors to stretch his legs and didn't seem to mind the rain in the least, although he did growl every time thunder rolled in from the horizon. Zak and I followed from a distance as he ran around sniffing everything in sight. It always made me happy when he was happy, but I hoped he'd take care of things quickly this evening. I had the hood of my waterproof slicker over my hair, but there was still rain running off my head onto the saturated ground below my boots.

"I bet there's a gorgeous view when the sun is out," Zak commented as we looked out over the raging sea. It was so dark that we couldn't actually see the water, but the sound of waves crashing on the rocks below left no doubt that the ocean was nearby.

"Maybe it will be sunny tomorrow. I heard one of the others mention that the castle has a stable that allows guests to borrow horses to ride on the beach. I've always wanted to ride a horse on the beach."

"I'm afraid the forecast is for rain for at least another twenty-four hours," Zak informed me. "But maybe it will clear by Saturday. I wonder how long it takes for the water to recede enough to open the bridge once the precipitation stops."

"With the ocean literally at the back doorstep of the castle, I bet it runs off pretty quickly. It's a good thing the castle sits up here on the bluff, however. Based on the sound of the waves I bet they'll be huge tonight."

I pulled my rain slicker more tightly around my body as the wind began to pick up. "I think Charlie has had enough time to do what he needs to do. Let's head in before the lightning in the distance makes its way onshore."

"Good idea."

"Charlie," I called as I peered into the distance. He'd been just a few feet in front of me a minute ago, but now I was unable to see his furry little body. "Charlie," I called louder.

The wind had picked up to the point that my voice didn't seem to carry at all. I cupped my hands around my mouth and called for my little buddy as loudly as I possibly could. He couldn't have gotten too far away in such a short amount of time, but even though I looked in every direction, I couldn't see him.

"Where could he have gotten off to?" I asked Zak, who was looking around as well.

"I don't know, but he couldn't have gotten far. He probably just can't hear us over the wind and waves." Zak cupped his hands around his mouth and called for Charlie.

I stood perfectly still and continued to look around the area. It was dark and becoming darker as the velocity of both the wind and the rain increased. Charlie was a light-colored dog and he had a flashing green light on his collar that usually could be seen from quite a distance. I have to admit I was beginning to get more than just a little bit worried.

"You don't think he got too close to the edge?" I said with fear in my voice.

"No. He's too smart for that. Charlie!" Zak yelled again.

I heard the faint sound of a bark in the distance. "He's over there." I pointed toward a small cottage that was most likely used as a guesthouse, or perhaps it was a groundskeeper's residence.

Zak and I hurried toward the building, which was actually farther away than it initially appeared. Like the castle, it was a stone structure, just a lot smaller.

"Charlie," I called again as I got closer.

Charlie continued to bark but didn't come as I commanded. Charlie was well trained and usually obedient, except when...

"You don't think—" I commented as I picked up my pace.

Zak, who had longer legs and therefore beat me to the cottage, stopped walking and knelt down. I immediately saw a body lying on the ground near the front door of the small cottage.

"Is it?" I asked.

"It's Brent Silverwood."

"Is he dead dead or fake dead?"

"I'm afraid he's dead dead," Zak answered.

To my mind, Brent had been a likely candidate for the role of the fake body, but who would want to kill him for real?

"Are you sure?" I found myself asking.

"I'm sure." Zak leaned away from the body. "It's raining hard enough to have washed away most of the blood, but if you turn him over there's a large pool of blood beneath the body."

Brent was lying facedown. Based on the blood on his shirt, it appeared as if he had been shot in the back.

"Should we call someone?" I whispered

"The bridge is closed," Zak reminded me. "We can't get off the island, but the local law enforcement can't get onto the island either." Zak tried the door to the cottage. It was open. "The water level in that creek over there is really coming up. I'm afraid if we leave the body where it is it could get washed out to sea. Let's drag the body inside and then head back to the castle to fill in Lord Dunphy."

Zak and I pulled the body into the cottage and then tossed a blanket we found over the top of it. We then closed the door, grabbed Charlie, and headed back toward the castle. When we arrived there, we were greeted by Byron, who was speaking to a man I assumed was the butler. We asked to speak to Lord Dunphy but were informed that he had retired for the evening and could not be disturbed. We filled the men in on what we'd found and then went in to our own room. Zak started a fire in the old stone fireplace while I drew myself a hot bath. If there was one thing I'd already learned about centuries' old castles it was that they were cold and drafty.

By the time I finished my bath the fire had warmed the bedroom and Zak, my poor, tired husband, was sound asleep in the big antique bed. I tossed my robe at the foot of the bed and was preparing to slip in next to him when I heard a humming sound that I couldn't identify. I wondered if it was coming from the bathroom, so I changed direction and headed back inside to look for the source of the sound, which had since stopped. The tub had emptied, the toilet wasn't running, and the sink was empty. It must have been something in the walls, or perhaps even something coming from the exterior of the castle. I stood quietly and listened, but the sound was gone.

I returned to the bedroom and was preparing, once again, to climb into the big bed when I noticed my robe was no longer lying across the end of the bed. I looked around the room to find it lying on one of the chairs that was situated in front of the fire. I glanced at Zak, who was still snoring softly. He hadn't moved since the first time I began to approach the bed. Charlie was still curled up in the same spot next to Zak.

"Catherine?"

Chapter 2

Friday, February 12

When Zak and I came downstairs the next morning everyone knew Brent was dead. I assumed the staff members we'd spoken to the previous evening had, at some point, filled Lord Dunphy in on the murder. I'm not sure what I expected the mood of the group to be once everyone found out, but I know I expected it to be different from the general atmosphere of excitement that greeted me when Zak and I joined the others for breakfast.

"I'll grab us some plates if you want to get a couple of cups of coffee," Zak offered. The meal had been set up buffet style. "I'll meet you at our seats."

I agreed to the plan and headed over to the coffee table, where the cook was refilling the coffee urn.

"Has Lord Dunphy come down this morning?" I asked.

"No, ma'am. The phone lines are down and the cell service isn't working on account of the storm. He is trying, unsuccessfully I believe, to reach someone via an old ham radio system he has in the workroom."

"I'm sure he wants to inform the authorities that a murder has occurred."

"Yes, ma'am, I believe so."

I poured two cups of coffee after the cook finished replacing the supplies she'd brought out from the kitchen. "Have you heard how long the storm is supposed to last?" I asked.

"I believe through the weekend, although there should be a temporary clearing on Saturday. I hope the forecast is wrong and the weather clears sooner, but I'm not holding out much hope because it seems to have intensified since last night."

I nodded. "When I took my dog Charlie out this morning even he was reluctant to venture into the sheets of rain. I noticed that all the small tributaries are spilling onto the grounds. It seems like the castle is almost completely surrounded by water."

"It gets that way at times. The outbuildings will most likely flood, but the castle was built up on the highest land mass in the area. We will be fine." The woman glanced around the room, as if looking for someone. "I should get back to the kitchen. Let me know if you need anything else."

"I will. And thank you. The food looks delicious."

I glanced toward the buffet table, where Zak was chatting with Armand. Both men were frowning, which I assumed wasn't a good sign. I continued over to the dining table with the coffee and sat down across from Millie. Apparently Piper hadn't come downstairs yet.

"I guess you heard we had a real murder," Millie informed me.

"Yes, I heard."

"I was afraid this weekend was going to be boring, but a real murder... Now, that is something I can get excited about."

I frowned. I got that Millie didn't personally know Brent, so I guess I could understand why she might not be experiencing distress at the man's passing, but the glee she was exhibiting was just wrong.

"Have you heard whether there's a suspect?" I wondered.

"I haven't, but as far as I'm concerned, until I sort out all the clashing energies in the castle, everyone is a suspect, including the ghosts."

I did remember that Lord Dunphy had mentioned conflicting auras the previous day and had to wonder if Millie was picking up on something similar.

"Clashing energies?" I asked.

"Everything is inside out and backward. What we see is not what we know."

"We?"

Zak joined me and Millie turned her attention to Cassandra, thereby putting an end to the conversation before she answered me. Who was this *we* she was talking about?

"Everything okay?" Zak asked. He must have noticed my frown.

"Yeah, everything is fine. I spoke to the cook and she said the storm is predicted to continue through the weekend."

"Armand mentioned that as well. I've been thinking about the location of Brent's body in relation to the flooding. Based on the amount of precipitation this morning, it seems obvious to me that if we hadn't found Brent's body last night it would have washed away and ended up in the ocean at some point during the night."

"Do you think someone intended that to happen, figuring that no none would come along and find it during the storm?"

"Maybe. But if that had been the intent I'm not sure why the killer wouldn't have just dragged the body to the cliff and tossed it over."

"Do you think Brent was killed in the spot where we found him?" I asked.

"It would be my guess that he was based on the amount of blood beneath the body. If he had been washed out to sea the blood his body was protecting would have washed away as well. It's doubtful anyone would ever have discovered what had become of him."

"So maybe the killer was unable to move the body for some reason," I suggested. "Brent was a large man. A small killer, like say Piper or Millie, might not be able to drag a man of his size and weight to the edge of the bluff. Perhaps they realized Mother Nature would take care of disposing of the body in a few hours and simply left him where he fell."

Zak took a sip of his coffee. "I suppose if that were true it would narrow down our suspect field, although neither woman seems the type to kill a man in cold blood."

Piper wandered into the room along with Jessica, so Zak and I paused our conversation until we were alone. At this point no one was talking about the game, which I assumed would be canceled, because everyone was talking about Brent's murder. Chances were the killer was in the room strategizing and building theories with everyone else. I decided it gave him or her a distinct advantage to know what everyone was thinking. Zak and I were going to keep our own ideas to ourselves for the time being.

I noticed Armand sat down at the opposite end of the table with Sam and Luke. I figured it was best to divide and conquer, so I nodded for Zak to join the men. Luckily, he understood my unspoken request, picked up his plate, and moved to the other end of the table. I looked around the room, taking a mental roll call as I did.

Piper, Millie, Jessica, and Cassandra were all sitting near me, Sam, Armand, and Luke were chatting with Zak, which left Susan and Drew unaccounted for in terms of the guests.

Turning to the staff, the cook had said Lord Dunphy was in the workroom trying to establish communication with the outside world, and both the cook, whose name I'd learned was Bonnie, and Byron were in and out of the kitchen, bringing out more food. I hadn't seen the maid who had been on the premises when we first arrived or the man we'd spoken to the previous night.

At this point I supposed the killer could be anyone. The main question in my mind was what Brent had been doing at the cottage in the middle of a rainstorm in the first place. I remembered he'd left dinner to take a call, or maybe it was to make one. It was possible someone could have arranged to meet him at the cottage for one reason or another. The lack of lines on my own cell confirmed that service was still out, but perhaps we could find Brent's phone and look up his recent call history.

Looking back, perhaps Zak and I should have looked around a bit better after we'd found the body.

"So, what do you think?" Piper asked me.

"Think?" I really hadn't been listening to the conversation going on around me.

"About putting together a card tournament of some type this afternoon. It's clear the rain isn't going to stop, which is too bad, actually. There is a lovely little footpath leading from the castle down to the most beautiful beach. Poppy and I spent quite a bit of time walking along the waterline when we were here last summer."

"A card game sounds good, although other than poker and old maid my card-playing repertoire is pretty limited. Still, I'm willing to learn."

"Perhaps bridge," Jessica suggested.

"Or canasta," Cassandra countered.

The discussion of which card game would make for the best tournament continued and I once again tuned out. The man who had been with Byron in the hallway the previous evening came in. He said something to Byron and the two men hurried away. They had a look of urgency about them, so I decided to follow them. I excused myself from the women and scurried off in the direction I'd seen the men take. At first I thought I'd lost them, but then I heard the sound of voices from below and realized they'd gone down into the workroom. It took me a few minutes, but eventually I found the entrance and, as quiet as a mouse, I tiptoed down the stairs.

"What do you mean he's gone?" Lord Dunphy shouted.

"I went to the cottage to check on the victim, but there was no body," the man who was not Byron explained. "The place is clean. If there ever was a body, there isn't a sign of it now."

"Have the two of you been keeping an eye on the guests as I asked you to?" Lord Dunphy asked.

"We have. Neither of us has seen anyone leave the castle."

"Take a look around," Lord Dunphy instructed. "If there is a body it has to be somewhere."

"Yes, sir."

"And Liam…"

The man we'd assumed was the butler paused.

"Let's keep this between the three of us until we get things sorted out."

I quickly crept back up the stairs and hid in a small closet at the top while Byron and Liam hurried past. As soon as I was certain they were gone, I slowly opened the closet door and snuck back down the stairs. Lord Dunphy was still working on the radio. What I found odd was that he was having a conversation with someone, although as far as I could tell there was no one else in the room.

"I tried tightening the wires, but I'm still not getting a signal," Lord Dunphy said to the person I couldn't see.

"Yes, I tried that as well."

I took a silent step forward to see if I could identify the person his lordship was speaking to, but the room appeared to be empty.

"Of course I am concerned that a real murder has occurred. We both know this couldn't have happened at a worse time."

I watched as Lord Dunphy tossed the screwdriver he'd been using to work on the radio across the room in frustration. "Stop nagging me. I'm doing the best I can."

With that, Lord Dunphy stood up. I headed back up the stairs. I still hadn't seen or heard anyone, but his lordship seemed to be pretty mad at someone. Or perhaps something. Could he have been arguing with a ghost?

When I returned to the dining room Zak was gone, but Drew had shown up and was speaking to the other women. Susan was still missing. Of course based on her figure I was willing to bet she didn't eat breakfast, which led me to believe she was most likely sleeping in.

I decided to head back to our room. If Zak had left the dining room that was most likely where he had gone. If the castle really was now cut off from the rest of the world—and it appeared that was the case at least temporarily—it was time for Zak and me to get to work tracking down the killer. A man was dead, and I for one intended to find out who had killed him.

I found a note from Zak, saying that the rain had temporarily slowed and he was taking Charlie out to stretch his legs. The poor little guy had been spending a lot of time in our room. I pulled on my waterproof boots and slicker and headed downstairs and toward the exterior door. Zak was right; the rain had slowed to a light sprinkle, although the dark clouds on the horizon seemed to indicate that there was more rain on the way.

I could see the yellow of Zak's raincoat in the distance, so I headed toward the bluff. Even though Lord Dunphy's men had reported that the body was gone I figured it couldn't hurt for Zak and me to take a look for ourselves. I was willing to bet we had a lot more experience investigating murders than the men who worked at the castle did, which meant we might stumble across something they'd missed.

"Good; you found my note," Zak greeted me when I caught up with him. "I looked around and you were gone."

I explained about following the men into the workroom and the shocking discovery they had revealed to Lord Dunphy. I didn't mention the conversation I'd overheard between his lordship and what might have been a ghost. Zak never has said as much, but I don't think he believes in the existence of ethereal beings the way I do. He tends to depend on logic when viewing the world, where I like to delve into the realm of the possible.

"If someone moved the body we're going to have a heck of a time creating our suspect list," I concluded.

Zak frowned. "I guess we should have looked around a little more carefully last night."

"My thought exactly."

"The castle is filled with people chosen to be here because of their ability to solve crimes," Zak pointed out. "Doesn't it seem odd to you that we seem to be the only ones interested in investigating?"

"Maybe we *aren't* the only ones investigating. Maybe the others are keeping things to themselves the same way we are, although the women *were* arranging a card tournament for later."

"If I were the killer I might arrange something like that as a diversion to keep people occupied," Zak suggested.

I tried to remember who'd initially suggested the card game, but I really couldn't remember.

Once we arrived at the cottage we tried the front door, which was now locked. Figured. We didn't have any tools with us to pick the lock, so we decided to look around the building for another way in— perhaps a back door or an unlocked window. We walked around the building several times, but there was no way in.

"So what now?" I asked.

"Let's head back to the castle to find something to pick the lock. The next time we take Charlie out we'll be prepared."

"It's a good thing we have Charlie with us," I commented. "No one is going to question why we're going in and out all the time."

The rain began to pick up as we made our way back to the castle. Charlie was covered in mud, so I gave him a quick bath while Zak looked for something to use to pick the lock. I was just mopping up the puddle on the bathroom floor with the last towel when there was a knock on the door.

"Good day, ma'am," the maid I'd seen when we'd arrived said. "I ran into your husband downstairs. He said you would need additional towels."

"He was right." I accepted her offering.

"What an adorable dog."

"His name is Charlie. Come on in. Charlie loves meeting new people."

The girl, who walked with a limp even though she appeared to be a few years younger than I was, hesitated, but then continued on into the room. I shut the door behind her. Charlie loved her immediately, which was indication enough for me that she wasn't the killer. Charlie was an excellent judge of character.

"My name is Zoe."

"I'm Liza."

"Have you worked here long, Liza?"

"Since I was a wee girl. My father died when I was young, so my mother got a job working for Lord Dunphy. She continued to work here until she passed. It's hard to get by without a man."

"Yes, I suppose it is." I didn't necessarily agree, but everyone had a unique situation.

"She wanted me to be able to take care of myself, considering no man would marry me due to my gimp leg, so she got me a job here as soon as I was old enough. I've been here ever since."

"You think no man will marry you because you limp?"

"'Tis true. Men around here are looking for women who can bear their children and help work their farm."

I frowned. I was about to make a comment about life in the twenty-first century but decided to let it go. I really wasn't familiar with the Irish culture, so what did I know about what men would find as desirable traits in the women they courted?

"Are you an only child?" I wondered.

"Am now. I had a brother, Danny. He was a soldier. He died fighting for what he believed in a few years back."

"I'm so sorry. I know it's hard to lose someone you love."

"Yes, ma'am. It is. More than you can imagine."

I decided to change the subject before we were both in tears. What I really wanted to know about was the other employees in the castle.

"So if you've worked at the castle since you were young you must know Lord Dunphy fairly well?"

"Yes, ma'am. He is like family. Almost like a father since my own papa passed."

"And the other employees: have they all been here for a long time as well?"

Liza smiled as Charlie licked her cheek. "Bonnie, the cook, took over when my mom passed about three years ago. She brought Byron, the server, with her when she came. He only works when there are guests to tend to. Liam, the stable hand, has only just started. In fact, this is his first week on the job. The old stable hand had been here for over thirty years before he retired. I miss him quite a lot."

"Stable hand? I thought Liam was a butler or something."

"No, ma'am. Liam tends to the horses. He has a room out in the stable."

"I guess I just assumed he was one of the indoor staff because I saw him upstairs last night."

Liza frowned. "The man who tends the stable rarely comes into the castle when there are guests. He even eats in his room in the stable. I don't know why Liam was here last evening."

"So he would have been out in the stable the entire time we were having dinner and meeting in the parlor for drinks?" I verified.

"Yes, ma'am. That is where he should have been. The horses tend to get skittish when there is a storm such as this. Liam would have been on hand to calm them."

Which meant he could easily have killed Brent. If he was never in the castle, then he wouldn't have had to be indoors and then go out, risking being seen.

"I really should go," Liza announced. "Thank you for letting me pet your Charlie."

"The pleasure was all his. Stop by any time to say hi if you'd like."

"Thank you, ma'am. I'd like that very much."

I spent a few minutes cleaning up the room after Liza left. I piled all the dirty towels in one corner, wiped out the tub, and straightened the rugs that had been placed on the stone floor. By the time Zak returned Charlie was clean and sweet-smelling and the room had been returned to order.

"Did you know that Liam was the stable hand and not the butler?" I informed Zak.

"No. I assumed he worked in the house because we found him there last evening. Do you think the fact that we were mistaken is significant?"

"I spoke to Liza, the maid, when she brought the towels. Thank you for sending her up, by the way. Anyway, she said Liam has a room in the stable and he rarely comes inside when guests are here. It seems he even eats in his room. Which makes me wonder why he was not only inside the castle last night but upstairs where the guest rooms are located."

"Good question."

"Liam is also the person Lord Dunphy sent out to the cottage to check on the body this morning. If he's the killer, he either could have lied about it being gone or he could have moved it when he was supposed to be checking on it. I have no idea whether Liam has a motive to kill Brent, but he seemed to have both the opportunity to kill the man and to move the body without drawing suspicion based on his movements."

"Okay, so what do you suggest? It would be suspicious if we headed back outside again so soon. Everyone knows I just came back from a walk, and several people know you just gave Charlie a bath."

"True. But we can head back to the cottage when we do go out again, and we might want to swing by the stable as well. In the meantime we should move Liam to the top of the suspect list."

"We have a list?"

"Not yet, but we need one. Did you bring a notepad in your computer bag?"

Zak unzipped his bag, took out a pad, and handed it to me. The Internet, like the phones, was inoperable, which was too bad because I had a sudden urge to do background checks on everyone on the property.

I began to make a list of suspects. I put Liam on the top. Then I thought about the other employees. Liza didn't seem the type to be a killer and Charlie liked her, so I was pretty sure we could eliminate her. The cook had been in the kitchen the entire previous evening, so I doubted she would have had the chance to shoot Brent. Likewise, Byron had moved over to the bar after he'd finished serving the meal, so I didn't believe it could have been him. Lord Dunphy had left to go upstairs, so in terms of opportunity, it most definitely could have been him. Plus, he'd been in charge of inviting everyone. If he did have a motive to want to kill Brent, the party could very well be nothing more than an opportunity for him to get Brent to visit the castle. He had seemed surprised when he was informed that the body was missing. I put him on the list, but I didn't consider him a strong suspect. There were easier ways to kill a man than to throw a party for twelve people.

As for the guests, I knew Zak and I hadn't done it, so that left ten; nine when you eliminated Brent because I doubted he'd shot himself in the back. Piper had left the group early, as had Armand, Luke, and Susan. I put all four of their names under Liam's. I furrowed my brow, trying to remember the movement of the other guests. Jessica had been chatting with Sam. I couldn't remember either of them leaving, at least not while Zak and I were still downstairs. Millie had been chatting with Cassandra and Drew, and she'd left to go to the ladies' room at one point. I hadn't noticed she'd been away an inordinate amount of time, but I added her to the list anyway. I was pretty sure Cassandra had never left the room, but I wasn't so sure about Drew.

"Do you remember if Drew left the room last night?" I asked Zak.

"It does seem like she left and then returned. I was tired and not paying that much attention, so I can't say how long she was gone."

I put her on the list just in case. "So this is who I have: Liam, Lord Dunphy, Piper, Armand, Luke, Susan, Millie, and Drew. All of them were out of the room for some period of time. Millie and Drew were only away for a short while, so I sort of doubt it could have been either of them, but Lord Dunphy, Piper, Armand, Luke, and Susan all left us shortly after dinner and never returned, and Liam was never in the room with us. Or at least he shouldn't have been. That gives us six strong suspects. I suggest we begin there."

"Begin how?" Zak asked.

"I'm not sure. I guess our first step should be to get a look at both the cottage and Brent's room. If there really is a card game later, maybe we can uncover alibis for some of the others and whittle the list down a bit. The fewer suspects the easier it will be to figure this out."

Chapter 3

Zak and I decided to join different tables for the card tournament, which would give us the opportunity to engage in conversation with twice as many people. Our plan was to participate in the tournament until we felt we'd learned all we could and then lose a sufficient number of hands to be eliminated. Losing was going to be easy for me because I'd never played the game they'd chosen; it was going to be staying in long enough to find out what I hoped to discover that was going to be the problem.

"I'm fairly certain I had a visit from Birte last night," Piper informed me and the three other people sitting at our table. "I can't be certain, but I felt a definite energy in the room after I retired for the evening."

"There has been a disturbance in the overall energy in the castle," Millie added. "In my opinion we should expect the spirits who reside here to be restless."

"I'm certain my robe was moved last night," I contributed.

"Are you all serious about this ghost stuff?" Susan asked. "It seems a little far-fetched to me."

"I agree with Susan," Cassandra joined in. "I'm fascinated by the notion of ghosts in the castle, but I'm afraid the whole thing is poppycock. In fact, Aunt Jessica is beginning to think the entire weekend is nothing more than a ruse."

"A ruse?" I asked.

Cassandra glanced toward the table occupied by Zak, Jessica, Sam, Armand, Drew, and Luke. "She thinks the ghosts are as phony as the murder."

"Jessica thinks Brent isn't actually dead?" Piper asked.

"She does. I mean, really... What proof do we have? No one has seen the body. Sure, he hasn't been around, but this is a big place. He could be hiding out in another part of the castle."

"Zak and I saw the body," I countered.

"Yes, so you say, but what if the two of you are in on it?" Cassandra insisted.

"I assure you, we aren't."

"Maybe. But Aunt Jessica has been asking around. I think she's spoken to pretty much everyone in the castle and on the grounds and no one other than you and your husband has seen the body. Not even Lord Dunphy. The whole thing seems suspicious to Jessica and me."

I looked toward the other table, wondering if Zak was fielding questions about Brent Silverwood's demise just as I was.

"Cassandra has a point," Susan jumped in. "You and Zak are the only ones to have seen the body. How do we know you aren't lying?"

"I already told you, we aren't."

"Then maybe you're the killers. It does seem odd that the body just disappeared into thin air."

"You heard the body disappeared?" I asked Susan. I wasn't aware Lord Dunphy had made that bit of news public.

"Sam found out somehow. I'm not sure who told him, but he's been nosing around and he assures me his sources have confirmed that the body, if there ever was one, is simply gone."

If nothing else, this conversation confirmed what I suspected: the other mystery solvers *were* investigating the murder, the same as Zak and me.

"I haven't seen the body," Millie chimed in, "but I can sense that a death has recently occurred. My instinct tells me the newest spirit in the castle isn't haunting us and most likely won't appear, though he hasn't moved on."

"Brent's spirit is here in the castle?" I asked.

"Yes, I believe so. Although..." Millie frowned.

"Although what?" I prompted.

"Something is off."

"Off how?" I persisted.

"The spirit I'm picking up is all wrong."

Okay, this was getting confusing. "Wrong how?"

"Maybe Brent is just having a hard time with the afterlife," Piper suggested.

Millie closed her eyes, then hummed and rocked her body back and forth. Eventually she opened her eyes. "No. It's more than that. Either the spirit I'm picking up isn't Brent, or Brent isn't Brent."

"That is absolutely ridiculous," Susan said. "You don't all actually believe this nonsense?"

"I for one believe in the presence of ghosts among us," Piper asserted. "I've seen them. More than once."

"I'm with Susan," Cassandra countered. "This whole conversation is absurd."

Everyone glanced at me. It was obvious Millie believed in the undead; was I supposed to be some sort of tie breaker?

"I'm open to the idea, but as of this point I haven't had any proof of the existence of those who have passed residing in our realm."

"Maybe we should just focus on the card game." Susan sighed. "This discussion is giving me a headache."

It took me only a few more hands to lose my way out of the tournament. I felt as if I'd learned all I could and I was anxious to compare notes with Zak. It took him a little longer to lose in a way that didn't seem contrived because he was actually a savant of sorts when it came to card games, but eventually he managed to serve himself enough bad hands to join me in our room, where I was waiting.

"Let's head out and we can talk while we compare notes," I suggested. A glance out the window showed that the rain had slowed to a drizzle. It had been that way since we'd been there. It would rain cats and dog and then slow, only to pick back up a short time later.

"Good idea. Just give me a minute to change my shoes."

Charlie was running around the room wagging his tail. It was obvious he was more excited about the walk than either of us. I did feel bad that he'd spent so much time in the room, although we'd been here less than twenty-four hours. Seemed longer.

Charlie took off chasing imaginary rabbits the moment his little feet hit the wet dirt. There was no doubt about it; Charlie was going to need another bath when this walk was over.

I began by filling Zak in on my conversation with the women at my table, including the fact that Millie thought Brent's energy was off. Whatever that meant. I was pretty sure Zak sided with Susan and Cassandra on the whole ghost thing, but he's polite and didn't say as much.

"So how about you?" I asked. "Did you pick up any juicy tidbits?"

Zak scooped me up in his arms and carried me through a giant puddle that would have topped my boots but only covered his much higher boots about halfway. "The conversation at my table wasn't nearly as lively as yours," he began as he deposited me on the far side of the puddle. "Still, I did learn a few things."

"Such as?" I asked as I grabbed Zak's hand and continued to follow Charlie.

"It seems to me that Sam and Jessica might be working together. Or at least sharing information. Neither volunteered any information but both asked a lot of questions. And they kept glancing at each other. As if to gauge the reaction of the other regarding what had just been said."

"I had a feeling the first time we met them that they might know each other from before. I guess it makes sense for them to share information if they're both interested in solving the murder."

Zak veered to the left to avoid a section of ground that was completely flooded. If Charlie wasn't careful he was going to end up having to swim across some of the larger puddles. Of course Charlie had grown up at the lake and was an excellent swimmer, so although I kept an eye on him, I wasn't worried.

"And the others?" I asked.

"It seems Drew was brought to the castle by Lord Dunphy to write a series of articles about the murder mystery weekend that was supposed to take place. According to Drew, the castle is in a bit of a financial bind and Lord Dunphy hoped people would be willing to pay big bucks for a weekend such as the one Drew was going to write about."

"So he planned to host the murder mystery weekends as a tourist-based business?"

"So it seems. There's a rich investor who wants to buy the castle and the land it sits on in order to develop a high-end resort and is threatening to buy the loan that was taken out against the property by Lord Dunphy's father. Lord Dunphy of course wants to save the castle that has been in his family for centuries. The murder mystery weekend was the only thing he could come up with."

"Wow, I guess a real murder on the introductory weekend is going to put a damper on his plans."

Zak stopped walking when we came to the edge of the bluff. There was nothing but ocean for as far as the eye could see. It really was beautiful. I could see why a developer might think this a good location to build a high-end travel destination.

"If I had to guess," Zak answered, "Lord Dunphy is probably pretty devastated by the way things have worked out, but Drew is thrilled. She came here to write a boring promo story and instead she lands right in the middle of a pretty spectacular murder. I mean, think about it: a Hollywood star is killed in the middle of a major storm in a haunted castle during a murder mystery weekend. It's gold and she knows it."

"Who exactly is Brent again?" I asked. "I know he was introduced as a movie star, but I can't think of a single thing I've seen him in, not that I go to that many movies."

Zak frowned. "I'm not sure what he's been in. I guess Dunphy never said. The name sounds familiar, though."

"Does it? I mean, Brent Silverwood sounds like a Hollywood sort of name, but can you really connect the name with anything Hollywood?"

"No, I guess not. I wish the Internet was up; I'd Google him."

I watched as Charlie changed direction and headed back toward us. As beautiful as it was overlooking the sea, I really wanted to check out the cottage, so I suggested to Zak that we head there.

"So, did Armand and Luke have much to say?" I asked as we walked toward the cottage.

"Luke didn't say a word, but Armand did share some of his adventures with us after Drew asked. He's lived a very interesting life. Not only has he taught at some of the top universities in the world, he's traveled extensively collecting rare artifacts."

"Lord Dunphy introduced him as a relic hunter."

"Yes, he did say that some of the items he has collected first had to be found and recovered. It really would be fascinating to travel the world in search of lost items from the past."

"I imagine it takes quite a bit of background knowledge to know what to look for and where to look for it," I commented.

"The man has definitely done his homework. He has an extensive education and it seemed obvious he's well read. He even knew quite a bit about the history of Dunphy Castle."

I stopped to call Charlie back. He'd seen something in the bushes and had taken off chasing it. "Tell me about the castle."

"It was first built in the fifteenth century by Aengus Dunphy. Most of the land in this part of the country belonged to him. He had seven sons, and the land was divided among them when he passed. His eldest son, Cronin, inherited this castle and the land it sits on. It seems the brothers didn't really get along and there ended up being centuries of feuding among Aengus's descendants for one reason or another. Armand didn't go into a lot of detail because we were supposed to be concentrating on a card game, but I take it that the wealth and influence of the Dunphy family dwindled in modern times to one lone castle and the few hundred acres it sits on."

"It would be interesting to do an in-depth study of the background of the place," I said as we approached the cottage. "If there are ghosts haunting this place and it's been around for six hundred years, you have to wonder how many ghosts actually reside here."

"Armand did say that there's been chatter over the years in some circles that Cronin Dunphy once haunted the place. Armand doesn't necessarily believe in the existence of ghosts, but Cronin was beheaded in the courtyard by his brother Malachi, who had fallen in love with Cronin's wife and challenged him to a sword fight."

"Ew. How awful."

Zak shrugged as he worked the lock of the cottage door. "It was a rougher time back then."

"Did Malachi take over as lord of the castle?"

"For a while. Cronin had several sons by the time he was beheaded. His eldest son, Orin, beheaded Malachi in an ambush several months after he moved in. Orin took the castle back, and it was Armand's belief that the current lord is directly descended from him."

The door gave way and Zak stepped aside. "After you, my lady."

I took my boots off, picked Charlie up, and stepped inside. I didn't want his footprints on the recently cleaned floor. That alone would make it obvious we'd been there.

I stood in the middle of the room and looked around. The cabin was clean and tidy. Too clean. The table surfaces weren't even dusty, which they would have been if someone hadn't wiped the dust away within the last day or so. Liam was correct; someone had not only moved the body but cleaned the place as well.

"Where should we start?" Zak asked.

"I'm not sure." I handed Charlie to Zak and then bent down to kneel on the floor in the spot where we'd left the body. The floor was made of stone, easily cleanable, and Brent had already bled out by the time we came across him. Whoever moved him had done an excellent job cleaning up after themselves. There was absolutely no evidence that anyone had been here.

"I still keep coming back to the question of why Brent was here in the first place," I commented. "It was pouring rain, so I doubt he was out for a stroll. He must have been meeting someone, but who and why here?"

Zak looked around the room. "It looks like a good place for a clandestine meeting between a man and a woman. Brent was here alone, and he appeared to be a young, single guy."

"So who was he meeting?" I mentally ran though my list of female suspects. "Piper and Susan were the only two who were out of the room when Brent left to make his call. Piper is much too old for Brent and Susan was with Luke."

"Was she?" Zak asked.

Actually, I didn't know if Susan and Luke were together or not on the night of the murder. I'd witnessed them sizing each other up, and they'd both excused themselves after dinner, but that didn't prove they'd hooked up once they left the group. The hookup was strictly supposition on my part.

"I guess we really don't know that for certain," I admitted. "Based on the timing of their departure from the group I guess I just assumed. Do you think it could have been Susan?"

"I suppose it's as good a theory as any, although all we have is a theory. We don't even have motivation. Part of the problem is that I get the feeling that not everyone here is who they want us to believe. We really don't know anything about anyone.

Susan was introduced as Sam's assistant, but that isn't very much information. Sam works out of San Francisco, so we assumed Susan lives there as well. Brent is an actor so we assumed he lives in LA, but no one actually stated that he lived there. Maybe Brent and Susan knew each other before the weekend."

"It wouldn't hurt to talk to Lord Dunphy to see what he knows about each of the guests," I offered. "We probably should have done it in the first place, but to be honest I still had him on my suspect list."

"And you don't now?" Zak asked.

"Not if what Drew told you about Dunphy setting up the weekend as a way to generate income to save the castle is true. Brent's death has hurt Dunphy's chances of saving the land that's been in his family all these years. I really don't see that he had a motive."

"What about Drew?" Zak asked. "Other than Susan, she's the next best candidate to have arranged a hookup with Brent. You said she left for a period of time, although no one could remember how long she was away."

"Why would Drew kill Brent?"

"She came to the castle to do a fluff piece on a murder mystery game and ended up with a chance to write a career-changing exposé on the murder of a Hollywood star. I'd say that could provide motive."

"Maybe." I frowned. "It seems a bit far-fetched. Still, I agree she should stay on the list."

"Have we eliminated anyone from the list?" Zak asked.

"In my mind we've eliminated Lord Dunphy."

"Anyone else?"

I thought about it. It did seem to feel like we were spinning our wheels. Liam was still my number-one suspect, followed by Susan, if she and Luke hadn't hooked up. I hadn't established an alibi for Piper, but I really didn't think it was her. Millie didn't seem like the sort to kill a man, but she had made some interesting comments about Brent having odd energy, so I intended to leave her on the list for the time being. As for Armand, I couldn't see why a world-renowned scholar would kill a Hollywood actor, though stranger things had happened.

"No," I admitted. "The only person I feel confident in eliminating at this point is Lord Dunphy. I guess our next move is to have a chat with the guy to see what he knows."

"Do you still want to go check out the stable?" Zak asked.

"Might as well. I don't think there's much for us to learn here, and so far the rain seems to be holding off. Who knows when we'll get a clear spell again?"

I took one last look around the cottage. Based on the fact that Brent had been facing the door when he was shot in the back, I was going to assume he'd never made it inside. That would indicate that the killer had intended from the beginning to kill him as he approached. From the way he'd fallen, it seemed the killer had been hiding in the trees just beyond the clearing. The problem I had with the whole scenario was that the door had been unlocked when Zak and I arrived. Later, when we'd returned, it was locked. Was it normally unlocked and the killer had opened it, intending for Brent to meet him inside? Or had the killer locked it later, after removing the body?

I discussed this paradigm with Zak as we walked toward the stable. Could there actually have been two different people involved that evening, with the person Brent went to the cottage to meet being a totally different person from the one who'd shot him? It seemed like a long shot, but Zak agreed it was possible that someone was waiting inside the cottage for Brent and a different person came from out of the woods and shot him before he arrived at his destination. If that was what had happened, the person who was waiting inside might know who had pulled the trigger.

"Yeah, but why wouldn't the person in the cottage come forward?" Zak asked as we made our way along the narrow path that led to the stable.

"Fear. If they saw what happened they probably don't want the killer to know they saw it. We're trapped here at the castle. All of us. With a killer. There's no way to escape or to call for backup. If you think about it, we're all sitting ducks. I can imagine the person waiting inside the cottage, if there was someone there, would have hidden when Brent was shot and then returned to the castle after the killer left. Admitting to anyone that there was a witness to the murder wouldn't be a life-sustaining move."

Zak and I hesitated when the stable came into view. The horses must all be inside; I didn't see any in the pasture.

"How should we play this?" I asked.

"We'll just wander over to the barn and look around. If anyone asks, we were walking Charlie and decided to stop by to check out the horses."

"Okay; that sounds like a good plan." I slipped the leash on Charlie. He was a well-behaved dog in most situations, but I didn't want to run the risk of him getting too close to a horse's hooves.

The barn was warm and smelled of hay and wild grains. It was spotless, which led me to the realization that even if Liam was a killer, he was also an excellent stable hand. There were four rows of stalls with four stalls in each row, each containing a large horse. I didn't know a lot about horses, but it appeared that the stock was all from excellent lineage. If Lord Dunphy wasn't able to find the money any other way, I was willing to bet he could raise a few bucks selling off part of his stable.

"These really are beautiful horses," Zak commented.

"It'd be fun to ride on the beach. I hope the rain clears before we have to leave."

Zak and I continued to discuss horse riding, horse breeding, and horse care while we looked around, just in case anyone was watching. So far no one had appeared, which could mean Liam was elsewhere. On the other hand, if he was the killer he might just be watching us. We needed to figure out a good reason to check out the rooms in the back, where Liam lived.

"You know," I said, after winking at Zak, "I need to use the ladies' room. Do you think there's one on the premises?"

"I guess you could check out those closed doors at the back of the building," Zak answered a bit too loudly for it to be a natural response.

"I think I'll do that."

Behind the first door I found a storage closet. Behind the second door was a small room that contained a bed, a table and chairs, a mini refrigerator, and a microwave. I didn't want to get too nosy until I checked out the third door, which actually did lead to a bathroom.

"It looks like we're alone. You keep watch and I'll look through Liam's stuff," I suggested to Zak.

It didn't take long to search the small rooms. I didn't find anything that would lead me to believe Liam was the killer, although if he was, he most likely would have hidden any evidence of his crime elsewhere. I was about to leave when I heard Zak say something. I hoped he was speaking to Charlie until I heard a second voice answer him back. I peeked out the door and found Liam's back was toward me, so I slipped into the hall and then into the bathroom. I waited a few seconds and then made a very noisy exit from it.

"Wow, that's a lot better," I said as I pretended to notice Liam for the first time.

I explained about taking Charlie for a walk and needing to use the bathroom. Liam didn't say anything to indicate he didn't believe my story, but I suppose if he were the killer he wouldn't give himself away by making a big deal of the fact that Zak and I had stopped by.

Chapter 4

When we returned to the castle, I took Charlie to our room for yet another bath, while Zak went in search of additional towels and Lord Dunphy. We hoped we'd be able to set up an appointment with him to discuss the other guests. Not that he'd have any reason to share what he knew with us, though I can be pretty persuasive when I really need to be. If nothing else, if what we'd heard about his financial crisis was true, we might be able to bribe him.

I realized that figuring out who had killed Brent and then moved his body wasn't my responsibility, but I had to admit the events of the weekend so far had me intrigued. As wacky as Millie had turned out to be, my Zodar was telling me that she'd been spot-on with her assertion that things weren't entirely as they appeared to be. I really hoped Lord Dunphy would have some information that would help shed some light on the situation as a whole.

As it turned out, Lord Dunphy was nowhere to be found. According to the staff, he hadn't been seen since early that morning.

At least Zak managed to score some extra towels to replace the ones I'd used to bathe my furry little sidekick.

"Lord Dunphy is missing?" I clarified.

"I didn't say missing," Zak assured me. "I said he hadn't been seen since this morning. This is a huge castle. There's a very good chance he's simply off somewhere working to restore phone service."

"I guess you could be right." I began gathering the towels I'd used for Charlie's bath. "But it seems odd that he's not doing more to identify Brent's killer. I mean, think about it: We're all trapped on this island with whoever shot Brent. What if it wasn't personal? Do you think we're in danger of additional murders?"

Zak paused, I assumed to consider my question. "I suppose it's possible there's some sort of deranged killer on the loose, but my instincts tell me Brent was the killer's target. Chances are the rest of us are perfectly safe. Still, I don't want you to go anywhere alone, and we both should keep our eyes open for any subtle clues as to what's really going on."

"Agreed. So what now? It's hours until dinner."

"Perhaps a nap." Zak wrapped his arms around me.

"I'm filthy."

Zak's grin was even bigger.

I laughed. "From the mud outdoors."

Zak kissed me quickly on the lips and took a step back. "Yeah, me too. I guess Charlie isn't the only one to need a bath."

"It's a pretty big tub," I commented.

"I like the way you think, Mrs. Zimmerman."

An hour later Zak and I sat on our bed dressed in clean sweats as we tried to sort out the difference between what we knew and what we suspected.

"Right now we have seven suspects," I began. For some reason I had all this nervous energy in spite of our very relaxing bath. I found myself rapidly clicking my pen open and closed as I spoke. "Liam, Luke, Armand, Piper, Millie, Susan, and Drew were all away from the rest of the group for a period of time, giving them all opportunity to varying degrees. As far as we know, Liam was never there, and Luke, Armand, Piper, and Susan left the group shortly after dinner. Drew and Millie were with the group for most of the time but left at some point, making it possible if not probable they killed Brent."

"Maybe we should work on eliminating those we think are the least likely candidates. At least we'd have a shorter list to work with," Zak suggested.

"Okay, I guess that would be Drew and Millie because they were with the group the majority of the time, and Piper, because I really don't think she did it."

"I saw Drew in the study working on the computer when I was looking for Lord Dunphy," Zak volunteered. "I'll go strike up a conversation with her. I haven't seen Piper, but Millie is in the arboretum doing yoga. Maybe you can start with her."

"That sounds like a good plan. We'll meet back here when we're done."

Now here's the thing about Dunphy Castle. It was built centuries ago and had managed to maintain its old-world charm. The floors and walls were made of stone, and the draftiness you'd expect from such a structure had been more than evident during our stay. Almost every room had a fireplace, which was the primary source of the heat in the huge structure. The castle had a moat, which was currently flooded, medieval weaponry on the walls, and a long, winding staircase leading to the roof.

But modern plumbing and electricity had been added over the years. And the kitchen...well, let's just say the kitchen is more elaborately outfitted than many of the world's finest restaurants. If Lord Dunphy was struggling financially, as we'd heard, I had to believe that was a relatively new development.

I bring this up because the arboretum, which I was heading toward, was like nothing you'd expect to find in an old stone castle. Based on what I've heard from the others, Lord Dunphy's grandfather had built the arboretum for his wife, who was ill and unable to go outdoors. It's one of the most awesome rooms I've ever seen, with a variety of plants and trees, a trickling waterfall, and climate control to ensure blooming flowers year-round.

As Zak had informed me, Millie had a mat laid out in front of the waterfall and was practicing a fairly difficult yoga routine. I didn't want to disturb her, so I took a seat on a nearby bench and watched the rain through the windows that completely encircled the room. It was pretty awesome to have the comforts that came from being indoors while enjoying the wide-open feeling of the outdoors.

Lord Dunphy's grandfather must have loved his wife very much if the thought that went into this room was any indication. It was obvious great attention had been paid to even the smallest detail to make the room a magical place in which to spend time.

Based on what I'd heard, it hadn't sounded like his parents had been very happy, and by all accounts it didn't appear the current Lord Dunphy was involved in a romantic relationship. There was of course the remote possibility that he really was hooking up with Piper. I wondered if the love Lord Dunphy's grandfather had demonstrated for his grandmother was the exception in the Dunphy family line. It didn't sound like things usually started off very well in terms of happily ever after in most of the Dunphy generations.

"Zoe. I'm sorry I didn't see you, dear."

Millie rolled up her mat and headed toward me.

"I didn't want to disturb you. You're very good."

"I practice every day. I find that yoga helps to keep my energy pure."

I smiled.

"Is there something I can help you with?"

"I wanted to follow up with you concerning our discussion this morning," I answered.

"Oh. What part?"

"The part where you said that Brent didn't seem like Brent. What did you mean by that?"

Millie sat down on the bench next to me. She paused before answering. I supposed she was choosing her words carefully. "People have an energy that's unique to them. Most don't notice it, but to me it's like a fingerprint or a signature. It's part of who they are, and most of the time it's congruent with what I know about them. I've found that certain types of energies seem to fit different profiles. Most of the time if someone is lying about something major such as who they are or what they do for a living, I can tell because their energy won't be consistent with their story. I could tell the minute I met Brent that something was off. His energy was all wrong. He was acting in a way that didn't demonstrate his true character."

I had to pause to let that sink in. What Millie was saying was sort of out there; on the other hand, it made total sense. What if Brent wasn't Brent? What if he was someone else pretending to be Brent Silverwood, Hollywood actor? I'd been trying to establish a reason why anyone on the premises would want to kill a man who was here researching a part in a movie, but what if Brent was really here for a completely different reason?

"If you could tell who he wasn't can you tell who he was?" I wondered.

"It's not like I can provide a name and address, but I could tell that the man had a secret. More than one. In fact, it seemed as if he was the sort who monitored very closely what he shared and who he shared it with. If I had to guess, he was a man who, rather than living in the spotlight, was used to living in the shadows."

"In the shadows? Do you think he was wanted by the law?"

"Perhaps. It's hard to say."

That certainly gave me something to think about. If Brent wasn't Brent, we would need to look at a completely different set of motives.

"You left the lounge last night for a short period of time. Did you see anyone else in the hallway?"

"No, I didn't, and if you're wondering, I didn't kill Brent."

"I didn't think you did."

Millie smiled at me. "Remember, I can tell when people are lying."

"Okay, I did suspect you a tiny bit. It's just that when I spoke to you this morning, you seemed so excited to have a real murder to investigate. It seemed really out of character based on what I'd observed about you so far."

"You must have spoken to Molly."

"Molly?"

"My other personality. She mostly stays in the shadows, but every now and then she likes to poke her head out and chat someone up."

"You have two personalities?"

"Certainly. We all have multiple personalities. It's just for most people, our alter egos stay tucked inside."

I know my face must have conveyed the fact that I thought the woman was crazy with a capital *C*.

"Haven't you ever acted out of character?" Millie asked.

"I guess there was a time or two in my youth when I might have had a tad too much to drink and a person who wasn't me in the least took over my body and went a little crazy."

"Really? Who was she?"

I frowned. "What do you mean?"

"This person who took over your body when you were drunk. If it wasn't you, who was it?"

"I didn't literally mean it wasn't me. I just meant that—" I stopped as it suddenly hit me. I totally got what Millie was trying to say. "It was me. Drunk Zoe was me; it just wasn't a part of me that I allowed to come out very often. Not at all, really, since I was a teenager."

"Exactly. Alcohol lowered your inhibitions and allowed Crazy Zoe to strut her stuff for a few hours. The thing is, Crazy Zoe is always there. She's a part of who you are even if you normally suppress her."

Wonderful. Just what I needed: a crazy alter ego waiting to burst forth the moment my inhibitions were lowered.

"Okay, I get what you're saying, but I don't give my crazy side its own name, and I remember what she did and said. Usually."

Millie laughed. "Don't worry; your energy is pure and free of fractures. While most people manage to find congruency between their selves, there are those, like me, who struggle with that congruency, due, usually, to some sort of childhood trauma. I was badly abused as a child, and carefree Molly, who finds fun in any situation, even the most gruesome and painful, was my way of coping. If things got too intense Molly would take over until things settled down a bit. I've known of Molly's existence for quite some time. We've learned to coexist, although I do believe we have additional work to do to really find seamlessness. But that's a heavy subject, for another day. For now, just be assured that I didn't kill Brent and I'd bet my reputation on the fact that the man who died didn't make a living in Hollywood."

Well, that conversation certainly had turned out to be different than I was expecting. I spoke to Millie a while longer about her work with law enforcement and the crimes she'd helped solve. It really was fascinating to realize that someone could find a kidnapped child simply by holding an item belonging to that child. I supposed Millie was like a bloodhound who just needed a sniff to find the scent.

I hoped I'd have more time to chat with this fascinating woman before we left the castle, but Zak was waiting for me, so I said my good-byes and headed back to our room. Millie had given me quite a lot to think about. Too much. It felt like my head was going to explode.

By the time I got to the room Zak was back as well.

"How'd it go?" he asked.

"You first. I'm still trying to process everything."

"Okay." Zak sat down on the edge of the bed. "As I already told you, Drew confirmed that she was sent here by her editor to do a fluff piece on the murder mystery weekend in an effort to promote the idea to large companies looking for a unique corporate retreat. She also said she was unhappy with the assignment because she's been working hard to establish herself as a serious journalist; doing that kind of piece wasn't going to help her career in the least."

"Did she mention why, out of all the journalists in the world, she was chosen for that assignment?" I asked.

"She said her boss knows Lord Dunphy somehow, and he'd promised him coverage of the weekend as a favor. She's convinced her boss singled her out because he feels threatened by her aggression and wanted to knock her down a peg or two."

"Yikes."

"Yeah, yikes. Anyway, she also admitted that while she felt bad that a man was dead, she was over-the-moon hyped about being in the right place at the right time to nail this story. She seems to think it might be just what she needs for national exposure."

"So she has a lot to gain by Brent's death."

"She does, if she can figure out what's going on. At this point she's as lost and confused as the rest of us. She also has an alibi. She told me that she left the cocktail reception after dinner last night because she had a headache and wanted to take some aspirin. She said she went to the kitchen for a glass of milk to coat her stomach before taking the painkiller. I spoke to the cook, who was cleaning up during the time Drew went for the milk, and she verified that Drew had come in for the milk, just as she said she did."

"So we can eliminate Drew from the suspect list."

"And Millie?" Zak asked.

I looked at Zak. "Do you remember when we were seniors and a bunch of us had that crazy party at the beach?"

"Sure I remember."

"Levi brought rum punch and I got *so* drunk."

Zak smiled. "Yeah, you did."

"Do you think the person who went skinny-dipping in the lake and wore her bikini bottoms as a hat was really me?"

Zak laughed. "Of course it was you. It was just a you who wasn't restrained by your inhibitions and decided to have some fun. Why do you ask?"

"It was just something Millie said. Anyway, she didn't do it, so we can eliminate her as well."

"So now we're down to five. Maybe we can clear a couple of others at dinner. Piper and Susan should be there, as should Armand and Luke. I guess we'll need to track Liam down another time if the others alibi out."

Dinner that evening had quite a different tone from the previous one. For one thing, it seemed as if everyone was keeping secrets from everyone else. Not that the whispered conversations and sly glances were unexpected. A man had been murdered, and as far as everyone but the actual killer knew, everyone on the premises was a suspect.

As they were the night before, Bonnie the cook and Byron the server were on hand to make sure everyone had a wonderful meal. The food was excellent. I knew a light lunch had been served during the card game, but Zak and I had been outdoors snooping around rather than eating with the others, so we were starving.

All the guests with the exception of Piper had shown up for the five-course meal. I found it interesting that Lord Dunphy was also absent from the table. Byron announced that Lord Dunphy was dealing with flooding in the workroom and

Ms. Belmont was feeling under the weather and had chosen to have dinner sent up to her room, but I had my doubts on both counts. Based on the meaningful glances between the various guests, it seemed the others had their doubts as well.

Liam wasn't around, not that I expected to see him, and with Piper's absence the only suspects from our list who were present were Susan, Armand, and Luke. I was trying to figure out how to separate one of the three for a private conversation when Susan got up from the table and ran for the stairs.

"Oh, my," Armand said. "I hope she's okay."

"I'll check on her," I volunteered. I got up from my chair and headed toward the stairs. I wasn't certain which room was hers, but one of the doors was cracked open, so I assumed that was the one she'd run into. I knocked, but there was no answer, so I slowly let myself in. I wasn't certain I had the right room until I heard the sound of puking from the bathroom.

Several minutes later Susan emerged, looking pale and fragile.

"I knocked," I explained, "but there was no answer. I hope you don't mind that

I let myself in; I wanted to be sure you were okay."

Susan sat down on the edge of the bed. "I think I have the flu. I started feeling ill immediately after dinner last night and came straight up to my room. I was sick all night, so I slept in this morning. When I finally woke up I was feeling better, so I came downstairs to join the card game. I didn't want to risk eating anything until I knew for certain that whatever I had going on had passed, so I skipped lunch. I decided it must have run its course, but after eating the soup tonight I felt sick again."

So Susan hadn't been dallying with Luke or meeting with Brent the previous evening; she'd been in her room puking her guts out. I supposed that gave her an alibi for Brent's murder, but it didn't really answer the question of where Luke had been, or who, if anyone, Brent had been meeting. I offered to go to the kitchen for soda crackers and tea, just as Susan ran for the bathroom once again.

Susan had seemed fine during the card game. Not flulike at all. Could she have been given something to make her sick both the previous evening and then again tonight? It seemed likely, but I had no idea why. And because she was the only one to get sick either the cook or the server had to be in on it. Once I delivered the crackers and tea, I intended to find out who it was.

After I delivered the tea and crackers to Susan I returned to the kitchen. The main course had been served while I was away and the cook was putting the finishing touches on the dessert. Byron, the server, was nowhere in sight.

"I'm afraid you missed your meal while you were tending to Ms. Langtree," the cook observed. "Would you like me to make you a plate?"

I couldn't help but remember Susan's pale face and sunken eyes. "Maybe I'll just have a piece of fruit," I said as I took an apple from the bowl that was sitting on the counter.

"The poor dear. She must have a nasty flu to make her so ill."

I hadn't actually mentioned how ill Susan was when I'd come down for the tea and crackers, only that Susan was feeling under the weather and needed something to sooth her stomach. This of course made me suspicious of the cook right off the bat.

"I'm pretty sure, based on her symptoms, that Ms. Langtree has food poisoning."

I watched a look of shock and denial cross the cook's face. "Impossible. I use only the freshest ingredients."

"Is it possible someone could have slipped something into her food after it was prepared?" I asked.

The cook frowned.

"Specifically her soup?" I added.

"I don't see how. The only people with access to the food prior to serving it was myself and Byron, and I've known Byron a long time. He would never intentionally make someone sick."

"Where is Byron now?" I asked.

"Liam came to fetch him. Lord Dunphy needed help in the workroom."

"Has Liam been in the kitchen at other times this evening?" I asked.

"He's been in and out a time or two," the cook admitted.

"And how long have you known Liam?"

"Only a week. He's new to the castle."

I looked around the room. I didn't see a back door, but I hadn't seen Liam come in to fetch Byron, although I had been upstairs with Susan. I asked the cook about another entrance and she said there was a back hallway that led from the kitchen to the workroom stairs, which didn't pass through the dining room. I grabbed a dinner roll and headed toward the workroom. I was more convinced than ever that Liam was the killer; now I just needed to prove it.

When I arrived at the workroom it was completely empty. And it wasn't just empty; it was dry. There was no way it had been flooded recently. Someone, or maybe everyone, was lying. I just didn't understand why.

Chapter 5

Saturday, February 13

I leaned up onto my elbow and looked at the clock on the table next to the bed. It said it was 2:10 a.m., much too late for anyone to be up and about, but I was certain I'd heard footsteps in the hallway. Zak was sleeping next to me and Charlie was snoring at the foot of the bed as I grabbed my robe and slipped into the narrow corridor. It was dark, but I could just make out a form ahead of me. I wasn't sure who—or what—I was following, but my instincts told me to remain quiet and hang back as I slipped past the closed doors on both sides of the passage.

When the faint figure got to the end of the hallway, it moved down the stairs, across the main entry, through the dining room, and toward the kitchen. At some point I lost sight of the figure I was following, but when I arrived at the kitchen door, I noticed a sliver of light at the bottom of the door, indicating that a light was on inside.

I slowly opened the door to see Lord Dunphy sitting at the counter eating a sandwich.

"Ms. Zimmerman," his lordship greeted me. "I see Mother was successful in fetching you."

Mother? As in the woman who had been dead for ten years?

"I was really hoping to avoid this, but I'm afraid we need to chat," Lord Dunphy continued. "Please pull up a stool and have a seat."

I did as the man told me. He seemed to be in a somber mood, and the dark circles under his eyes seemed more prominent than they had been the previous evening. I had a million questions for him, which I intended to ask before I went back upstairs, but he said he wanted to speak to me so I decided to let him begin the conversation.

"When I arose this past morning I was informed by Byron that you and your husband had found Brent Silverwood dead on the stoop of the groundskeeper's cottage." Lord Dunphy spoke in an emotionless voice, as if he were simply reading directions of one sort or another. "Needless to say, I was horrified by the news. We have never had a murder at

Dunphy Castle in my lifetime, although they were quite common in years past."

"It was pretty shocking for Zak and me to find the body as well," I assured his lordship.

"I can imagine. Still, there seems to be cause on my part for concern as to the validity of the event. I had Mother fetch you so that we can discuss this murder you claim has occurred."

"Claim?"

"So far we have not found any evidence that a body ever existed. There is no sign of a struggle outside the cottage where the man was reported to have been shot, and there is no evidence within the interior of the cottage to suggest that a body was ever inside. I have spent the entire day searching every nook and cranny in the castle, as well as every inch of the island. No body has been found. The only conclusion I can come to is that there never was one to find."

"You think we're making the whole thing up?"

"The evidence would suggest that to be the case. Liam is certain the whole thing is a ruse and Byron refuses to choose sides, but the fact that you found a body that has since disappeared is somewhat hard to swallow."

"If we were making the whole thing up where is Brent? You said you searched the place and didn't find a body, but did you find Brent alive?"

"No," Lord Dunphy admitted, "we did not. His belongings are still in his room and it doesn't appear that he ever slept there."

I got up off my stool and began to pace, which is something I often do when I'm agitated. "I'll admit the fact that the body is missing is odd, but I can assure you that the very dead body of Brent Silverwood was found by Zak and me last evening. We moved the body inside the cottage so it wouldn't be swept away and came to inform you. We ran into Byron and Liam in the hallway. They informed us that you were unavailable. We explained what had occurred and they assured us that he would fill you in on the situation."

Lord Dunphy frowned. "You say you ran into Liam in the house?"

"Yes. He was in the hallway on the second floor, talking to Byron."

Lord Dunphy didn't respond, but I could tell by the furrowing of his brows that he was thinking things through.

"Don't you think it's odd that they didn't inform you of Brent's death until this morning?" I asked. "It seems like the murder of a guest would be cause to interrupt you, even if you had gone up to your room for the evening."

"Yes, I see your point."

"And it was Liam you sent to check on the body. Isn't it possible that he's the killer and he moved the body to cover up the crime?" I added.

"Why would Liam want to kill Mr. Silverwood?"

"I don't know. What do you know about Liam?"

Lord Dunphy sat back on the stool. "Not a lot. My stable hand retired recently and Liam applied for the job. He seemed to know a lot about horses and he was willing to work for a lot less than most. He hasn't worked here all that long—in fact only a week—but I've had no cause to regret hiring him. He is excellent with the livestock and he seems to be a hard worker. He was born and raised right here in Ireland. I really don't see what motive he would have had to kill a visitor from the United States."

"I don't know either, but at this point he seems the most likely suspect. There are, however, others to consider. How well exactly did you know Brent?"

"I just met him the night of the dinner."

I frowned. "So how did he come to be here?"

"His agent, a nice chap named Dugan Westerly, called to ask if one of his clients could come to the castle to do research for an upcoming role. I thought it would be good publicity, so I arranged for him to be here the same weekend as Ms. Belmont's guests."

"Ms. Belmont's guests?" I knew Zak and I had been invited by Piper, and Millie had as well, but I'd just assumed the others had been invited by Lord Dunphy himself.

"Yes, the murder mystery weekend was her idea."

I returned to my stool and sat back down. "Okay, let's back up a bit. You said the weekend was Piper's idea. How did the whole thing come about?"

Lord Dunphy got up and went over to the refrigerator. He took out a covered dish and offered me a slice of pie, which I accepted. I hadn't eaten much dinner and I was starving.

"Ms. Belmont and her husband have visited Dunphy Castle on several occasions. In fact, I believe it is the only place they stay when they are in the area. During their last visit I mentioned to them that I wasn't certain if I would be able to hang on to the castle because, thanks to mismanagement on my father's part, my financial situation had become quite desperate. Ms. Belmont suggested the idea of offering murder mystery weekends to high-end clients. I was a bit skeptical at first, but Ms. Belmont insisted it was a brilliant idea. She told me that she would make all the arrangements for a trial run, which was scheduled for this weekend."

"So she was responsible for inviting everyone who's here this weekend?"

"Yes, except for Mr. Silverwood, of course, and Miss Baltimore. I called in a favor from an old friend and arranged to have the event covered by the press. At the time I thought it would be a good way to launch the weekends, should this one work out."

I felt like the fact that Piper was responsible for inviting all the guests somehow changed everything. I just wasn't certain how.

"Do you know why she chose each particular guest?" I asked as I took a bite of the pie, which was quite delicious.

"I know what she told me. She thought the weekend would be a lot more fun if all the contestants had a background in solving mysteries. She told me, for example, that you were an amateur sleuth who she'd met while vacationing this past summer. She said you actually had solved a murder while on your honeymoon."

"Yes, that much is true."

"Apparently Professor Waller works with Mr. Belmont in some capacity. She explained that Mr. Waller finds and retrieves lost artifacts, so I assume he must have Charles fence them."

"*Fence* them?"

"Yes, I believe Mr. Belmont deals in the acquisition and sale of valuable objects."

I knew Charles and Piper traveled extensively; I guess I must never have gotten around to asking what they actually did for a living.

"And Jessica?"

"Ms. Belmont informed me that she is a huge fan of her books. She told me that she has read them all multiple times and had always wanted to meet the woman who managed to weave such complex tales time after time. I suppose she found this weekend to be the opportunity she'd been looking for."

I knew Millie was Piper's psychic, which just left Sam. Dunphy admitted he wasn't certain how Sam and Piper were acquainted, but he was on her original list so he went with it.

I had a lot of new information; now I just needed to process it. I still felt like Liam was the best candidate for the killer, but I've found in my past experiences that the killer rarely turns out to be my original suspect. It was best to keep an open mind as I continued my investigation. I asked his lordship where Piper had been all day and he claimed not to know. I couldn't tell if he was lying, but I didn't suppose it really mattered.

I was thrilled to find the sun shining through our bedroom window when I awoke the next morning, but I was less than thrilled to find both Charlie and Zak gone. I hated waking up alone. I hadn't meant to sleep so late, but between my late-night chat with Lord Dunphy and the tossing and turning I'd done trying to process everything after I'd returned to the room, it had been the early hours of the morning before I'd finally gotten back to sleep.

I sat up and looked around the room. It appeared Zak had straightened up. I was about to toss back the covers to get up when Zak and Charlie returned to the room.

"Good, you're awake." Zak kissed me on the lips and handed me a cup of coffee.

He had a plate with a muffin in his other hand. "Charlie and I have already eaten, so I brought something up for you. It looks like we're going to have a few hours of sunshine before the next wave of the storm rolls in, so I thought you might want to go for a walk."

"I'd love to go for a walk." I smiled as I sipped my coffee. "I wonder if we can get down to the beach."

"I actually spoke to the cook about that when I was fetching your muffin. She explained that the trail that runs directly from the castle to the beach is steep and will be impassable, but she gave me directions to access the beach through the boathouse at the other end of the island. It really isn't that much farther than the stable."

"Sounds like fun." I picked off a piece of the poppy seed muffin and put it into my mouth. "I bet a lot of cool stuff washed up during the storm. Who knows what we'll find."

"I'll bring a bag to put things in." Zak sat down on the edge of the bed. "Now that you've had your coffee and been fed, do you want to tell me where you went last night?"

"Sorry. I didn't know you even realized I was gone."

"I thought we agreed we wouldn't do any sleuthing alone."

"I wasn't sleuthing. Exactly. I heard a noise in the hall. I peeked out and saw a figure, which I followed. She led me to the kitchen, where I found Lord Dunphy having a sandwich. I stopped to chat with him for a few minutes."

I shared my conversation with his lordship while I finished my coffee and muffin. Zak agreed with my assessment that it might be important that it was actually Piper who was responsible for the guest list. I asked him if he'd seen her downstairs, and he hadn't. He'd had breakfast with Armand, who'd shared some more about his travels. Zak confirmed that Armand had been alone in his room after leaving dinner on the night of the murder, which didn't leave him with an alibi, although he also shared that the more he got to know the professor, the more certain he was that he wasn't the killer we were looking for. Zak had a pretty good gut instinct I'd learned to trust. If we eliminated Armand based on that instinct and Susan because she had been in her room tossing her cookies when the murder occurred, that just left Liam, Piper, and Luke. At this point my money was still on Liam.

After I got dressed, Zak, Charlie, and I headed downstairs and out the side entrance. It was a cold morning, probably no warmer than forty degrees, but the sun felt wonderful on my face. Based on Charlie's quick trot, it was clear he was happy the sun had decided to poke its head out for a few hours as well.

The sea in the distance looked calm today. Waves gently lapped toward the shore, causing a pleasant backdrop for the sound of the birds that had come out to feed on the fish that had washed up during the storm. The air smelled fresh after the cleansing rain, although I had a feeling once the sun hit the dead fish scattered on the beach, the scent in the air was going to be something else entirely.

Charlie raced back and forth in front of us as Zak and I walked hand in hand down the narrow path the cook had instructed him to take.

"Did you happen to notice if anyone other than Piper was missing from breakfast?" I asked conversationally. I'd pretty much narrowed down the suspect list to three, yet I still felt it prudent to keep an eye on the comings and goings of the others.

"I didn't see either Susan or Luke. Armand mentioned that Luke had gone out for a walk because of the break in the storm, and I assumed Susan was still sick."

"About that: She said she first became ill after finishing dinner the first night and was sick all night. She felt better the next morning and actually thought she'd recovered until she ate the soup last evening. Do you think someone could be adding something to her food to make her sick?"

"I suppose it's possible, but why would anyone do that?"

"I have no idea. And the logistics of something like that would be tricky unless it was either the cook or Byron doing the adding. The way she described her illness didn't seem typical of the flu."

"There are all kinds of flu," Zak reminded me.

"True. Still, my Zodar is telling me that there's something off about this whole thing. I just haven't figured out what yet."

Zak and I continued to discuss the various aspects of the investigation until we came to the wooden staircase that led down to the boathouse. We carefully made our way down and then let ourselves in through the side door, which the cook had assured Zak would be unlocked.

"There's no boat," I observed.

"The cook said Lord Dunphy doesn't own one. In fact, the boathouse has been nothing more than an access to the beach for over twenty years."

"I'm surprised the waves haven't destroyed it. They sounded pretty big the past couple of days."

"When we were at the top of the stairs I noticed that this part of the beach is protected by a reef. I imagine that's why the boathouse was built here in the first place."

I supposed that made sense. It really was a pretty cool old building, even if it was falling into a state of disrepair. Zak and I walked along the wooden decking, which, unlike the rest of the structure, looked to be brand new, as we made our way toward the door at the front, which would lead out onto the beach. The view was breathtaking. The tiny waves that rolled in from the open sea didn't at all resemble the giant waves I'd heard breaking in the background for the past two days. Charlie was in heaven, running up and down the beach, chasing the birds. It was nice to get outside for some fresh air and sunshine after days of rain.

We decided to walk down the beach back toward the castle, which could be seen high up on the bluff. It was beautiful here, but I had to admit the isolation of the castle when the bridge was out and the residents and staff were unable to get into town would get tiresome after a while. One of the things I love most about my own hometown was that you could enjoy the feeling of isolation yet still be close to town and neighbors.

"It looks like we aren't the only ones to decide to take advantage of the nice day," I commented as I noticed two people farther down the beach at the foot of the castle.

"It looks like Luke," Zak said.

"And Susan," I added. "I knew the two of them were making eyes at each other. If Susan hadn't been sick that first night, I bet they would have hooked up then, as I predicted."

"Should we turn around to give them some privacy?" Zak wondered.

"I can't see them any longer. It looks like they must have gone on around the bend. Let's go ahead and walk down to the bend, then turn around."

Zak and I continued to walk down the beach with Charlie, chatting about the magic of the scenery. It really was the best time we'd had since we'd been in the Emerald Isle. Blue skies, a calm sea, and plenty of sunshine: What more could you ask for?

"I wonder if we'll get cell service now that the storm has passed."

"You need to make a call?" Zak asked me.

"I just wanted to check on the kids. And Ellie. And the new math teacher we hired. I know it's only been a few days since we checked in, but now that I'm outdoors in the fresh air and not stuck in the castle, I find that I'm starting to wonder how everyone is doing back in Ashton Falls."

"Yeah," Zak agreed. "I've had the same thoughts. I left my phone back in the room, though."

"Me too. Maybe we can try making the calls when we get back. I guess we should turn around. It looks like we're about to run out of beach." I frowned. "I assumed the beach continued on around the bend, but it just ends where the cliffs begin."

"Looks like."

"So where are Luke and Susan? When we saw them they were about where we're standing now, but I don't see them anymore and they didn't come back down the beach, so where did they go?"

Zak looked around. "Good question. Maybe they headed up the trail that leads directly to the castle."

I looked up at the trail. It was steep and muddy. There was no way anyone was getting up or down that trail until it dried out a bit. The beach ended beneath the spot where the castle was located up on the bluff. If you continued on around the corner the sea came all the way up to the cliff face. There was no way Luke and Susan had continued on in that direction. That only left one option."

"There must be another way into the castle. Maybe a cave or a passage that leads down to the beach."

"If that were true why wouldn't the cook have told me about it?" Zak asked.

"Maybe she didn't know about it. Perhaps there's a hidden staircase. I bet there's an opening behind those shrubs."

I walked toward the dense shrubbery that grew at the base of the bluff. It took quite a bit of searching, but eventually I found a small opening that looked like the entrance to a cave. There was an iron gate across the entrance, although it was open, but it was dark and we didn't have a flashlight. Still, I could see enough from the entrance to realize that I'd found the dungeons. I assumed the cells hadn't been used in recent times, but it did make sense that a castle as large as this one would have been built to include a place to hold those who fell out of favor with the current lord.

"I bet if you continue on you come to a doorway leading into the old part of the castle," I postulated. The castle as it existed today was divided into the section that had been modernized and the one that had been closed off. From the outside it looked like the building could have housed over a hundred people at one time, but the majority of the structure wasn't used, left to weather the elements over the years. I would estimate that only about a quarter of the available space was utilized in modern times. "It'd be fun to look around some more. Maybe we can come back with a flashlight."

"I have one in my suitcase. Let's head back now. It looks like the next wave of bad weather is about to make its way onshore and I don't want to get caught in it."

Zak, Charlie, and I turned around and headed back down the beach. I hoped we'd find cell service had been restored when we got to our room. As interesting as this trip had been so far, thoughts of home were never far from my mind.

Maybe we could bring the kids to Ireland one day. Alex might only be eleven, but she seemed to be fascinated by anything having to do with history, and Scooter would think the suit of armor standing in the hallway near our room was awesome. The kids had been living with us for less than a year, but already I thought of them as family. Pi, the eldest of the three minors in our care, had recently turned seventeen and was looking ahead to college. Technically he was only a high school junior, but he was way ahead of his peers academically, so Zak was looking into the possibility of having him begin college as early as the following fall. I'd miss him, but I could see he was more than ready for that step.

"I wonder how Ellie is doing with Brady," I said aloud.

Brady Matthews was the new math teacher we'd hired for Zimmerman Academy, the private school we run, when our previous teacher, Will Danner, had left us after the New Year. Brady hadn't been able to make the move until this past week, so my best friend, Ellie Davis, had agreed to pick him and his three children up at the airport and get him settled into the house Zak and I had rented for him.

"I'm sure they're getting along fine. Brady is a good guy and my guess is that Ellie is having a wonderful time helping him get settled."

"You didn't hire him as a hookup for Ellie, did you?"

Ellie recently had broken up with her boyfriend and my other best friend, Levi Denton, and had been feeling a little lost since Levi had entered into another relationship almost immediately.

"Of course not," Zak denied. "I offered Brady the job because he was the most qualified of the candidates I interviewed. It did occur to me, however, that Brady was exactly what Ellie has been looking for."

Zak wasn't wrong. Brady was intelligent, kind, and easygoing. He was a widower with three young children, a daughter named Holly, who was four, and twin boys, Hudson and Haden, who were just eighteen months. It was hard to know how people would relate with each other when they actually met, but on paper, Brady was perfect for Ellie.

Chapter 6

Upon returning to the castle, we found cell service was still out, which was frustrating, but Zak thought now that the weather had cleared a bit, he might be able to get satellite service on his laptop. It looked like the clearing trend was temporary, so I left him to that while I cleaned Charlie up.

I'd noticed Piper sitting in the lounge when we arrived, so when Charlie was once again fluffy and sweet smelling, we headed back down to have a chat with her. If she was the one responsible for inviting all the murder mystery contestants, maybe she could provide me with the additional details I needed to try to make sense of everything that was going on.

I found Piper sitting by the fire reading a book when I entered the room. She smiled and motioned for me to have a seat on the sofa across from her.

"I missed you at dinner last night," I began.

"I'm afraid I've been a bit off my food since I've been here. I thought it might be the flu, but it seems to come and go."

Sounded like Susan's symptoms exactly. I had to wonder if there was a flu going around or something in the food.

"I take it you've been out investigating the murder," Piper continued.

"Actually, Zak and I just took Charlie for a walk, although I do admit to being curious as to what's really going on."

"Yes." Piper frowned. "I'm afraid having a real murder on the first night of a murder mystery weekend is not going to produce the results I'd hoped for."

"And what results are those?"

Piper leaned in, as if sharing a secret. "Between you and me, Lord Dunphy is broke. From what I understand, his current state of affairs is not his fault but rather mismanagement by his father, despite his mother's assistance. He happened to mention his situation to Poppy and me the last time we were here and I realized the man was sitting on a gold mine."

"A gold mine?"

"Not literally, dear. As far as I know there is no gold in these parts. The gold mine I refer to has more to do with the potential experience the castle has to offer its guests. Dunphy Castle has been operating as a lodging facility for quite some time, but his lordship really hasn't done anything to establish the castle as a unique destination. One of the reasons I so enjoy coming here is because of the possibility of running into one of the resident ghosts. The murder mystery theme seemed to fit with the haunted castle idea, so I proposed offering murder mystery weekends at five times the rate currently being charged for a room."

"And you think people will pay that?" I asked.

"I think they will if we do a good enough job of building the hype and creating a scarcity of reservations. Everyone loves a ghost."

I supposed that much was true. Zak and I had been invited here, but I would have paid quite a lot to experience a murder mystery weekend in a real haunted castle.

"So you invited people you knew?"

"Exactly. I figured we'd invite people with experience in solving one type of mystery or another to compete for bragging rights because his lordship can't afford a cash prize. I suggested to Fergus that we have the media cover the event. I thought a news story would create interest in the weekends. I hoped things would go well enough that he'd get reservations right off the bat."

"I know why you invited Zak and me, but can you share why you invited the others?"

Piper looked around the room as if to satisfy herself that we were truly alone. The entire exercise seemed ridiculous, given the fact that I hadn't asked for her country's secrets but simply inquired about the guest list. I'll admit that having a real murder occur in a haunted castle during a storm had provided just the right atmosphere for us all to feel as if we were characters in one of the mysteries I knew Piper was fond of.

Piper lowered her voice before she began. "Jessica Fielding is my favorite mystery writer. Not only are her stories complex and well thought out but she is such an interesting person. It seems that she stumbled across the answer to a decades' old cold case several years ago while doing research for one of her novels. After she was able to prove her conclusions to local law enforcement, and the killer was apprehended after almost getting away with a perfect murder, she became intrigued by the process. She has investigated and tried to solve several other crimes in her spare time. I'm not sure her current endeavors have met with the same success she realized the first time, but she has made progress in several different cases. Her approach to the whole thing captured my imagination. I've always wanted to meet her and saw this as an opportunity. I know she isn't a real detective, but she has had some luck with her cold cases, so I thought she could give professionals such as yourself a run for their money."

"I'm not a professional."

"You might not get paid for what you do, but I consider you a professional all the same."

I smiled. She was laying it on pretty thick, but I didn't mind. My ego could use a boost right about then.

"And the others?" I asked.

"Armand is a friend of Poppy's. In fact, Poppy suggested I invite him."

"Lord Dunphy told me Charles sells the artifacts Armand finds."

"Some of them. Certainly there are those that end up in museums. But if Armand finds a rare object that doesn't possess any specific historical value, Poppy helps him out."

"So Charles is an antiquities dealer?"

"You could say he's a matchmaker of sorts."

"A matchmaker?"

"If someone has an expensive piece of art or a rare artifact to sell, Poppy matches them up with a buyer. Poppy and Armand have worked together several times and have become friends."

"Do you know why Charles suggested Armand for this specific weekend when he himself isn't here?" I asked.

Piper frowned. "Charles knows Armand well enough to realize that he would enjoy such an opportunity and suggested that I offer him an invite. I'm sure the opportunity to stay in the castle was welcome. It certainly holds a lot of history within its walls. In fact, Armand has been holed up in the library almost since we've been here. I popped my head in to say hello when I came down today, but he was so interested in the books and documents he had spread all over the table near the fireplace that he didn't even hear me."

"Do you know what he's looking for?" I asked.

"I'm afraid I don't. You can ask him if you can get his attention."

Doing just that was going to be my next stop.

"And Millie is your psychic," I verified.

"Yes, dear."

"And Sam?"

Piper furrowed her brow. "Sam was referred to me by Armand, who I believe got his name from Luke. I'm not sure how the men know each other, but Armand knew I wanted a fifth and he gave me Sam's contact information."

"Luke and Susan are both here as guests, but they seem to be spending time together. Do you happen to know if they knew each other prior to this event?"

"Not that I know of. Still, Susan works for Sam, who was invited after Luke provided his name to Armand, who passed it on to Charles, so it stands to reason that Luke and Sam know each other. I suppose that can lead to an inference that Luke and Susan know each other."

Made sense.

"And you had never met either Brent or Drew before this weekend?"

"No. Fergus told me Brent's agent called to ask that he be included and, as I indicated, Drew was invited as a result of Fergus calling in a favor so that we would have media coverage. It really is a shame the way everything turned out. I think we would have had a wonderful weekend if not for the fact that we had a real murder." Piper frowned. "Do you know if they ever found the body?"

"Not as far as I know."

"It does seem odd that the body simply disappeared. I asked Fergus about it and he is as stumped as I am. This is a large castle, though, so I'm sure there are many good hiding places should someone desire to hide something."

"It occurred to me that the killer might have dumped the body in the ocean."

Piper shook her head. "The same thing occurred to me, but Fergus said the way the tides work around the island, anything that is swept out to sea on one part of the beach turns up on another."

"Zak and I were just down on the beach and we didn't see anything, although we didn't walk all the way around the island. Did you know that there are dungeons beneath the castle?"

"Indeed I did. They haven't been used in a century, but they've been left undisturbed, so I imagine there is quite a bit of history that could be learned from within these walls. You should have Fergus tell you some of the tales that have been passed down. They are really quite fascinating."

I was sure they were both fascinating and horrifying. I couldn't imagine the living conditions the dungeons suggested. I was sure there were people who were simply left there to die.

"Do you know if there's a passage that leads to the dungeons from inside the castle?" I asked.

Piper frowned. "Not that I am aware of. When Fergus showed them to me it was from the entrance on the beach. Still, it would make sense that there would be a way to access the area from inside the castle. Perhaps you should ask him that as well."

I decided to start my inquiries with Armand because I knew he was in the library and I had no idea where Lord Dunphy might be. As Piper had indicated, Armand was sitting at a table that was completely covered with books and yellowed documents. He didn't so much as look up when Charlie and I entered. The library was a large room with a high ceiling. Almost every wall was lined with bookshelves that reached from the floor to the ceiling. There had to be tens of thousands of books in the room. Many appeared to be old, although there were clearly modern titles along one wall as well.

It was a cheery room with a large fireplace, overstuffed sofas, hardwood tables and chairs, and a large woven rug covering the middle of the floor. There were large portraits on either side of the fireplace, which I assumed were paintings of previous lords of the castle. In that moment I felt like I truly had stepped back in time. It was really an awe-inspiring feeling to know that people had stood in this very room centuries before I'd even been born.

"What a great room," I said to Armand as I sat down across the table from him.

He looked up. I could tell by the surprise in his eyes that he hadn't realized I was in the room until I had spoken. Talk about being focused on your work.

"Ms. Zimmerman, how are you?"

"Zoe, please. And I'm fine. It looks like you've found a project to occupy your mind while we wait for the bridge to reopen."

"Indeed I have. I must say I was pleasantly surprised by the number of old books and documents contained in the castle. If I had known the treasure I would find, I would have visited earlier. Much earlier."

"Are you researching anything specific?" I asked as Charlie settled in front of the fire.

"Not really. I started out reading an old journal, which left me with some questions. I then sought out specific books and documents in an effort to answer those questions. One question led to another, and at this point I'm simply taking in as much history as I can. It's been a wonderful experience. I'm a historian and I've spent a lot of time in dusty old libraries, but I must say I've loved each and every one of them. Each book, each document, every library, and every old building has a unique story to tell. I'm hoping Lord Dunphy will allow me to stay on after the bridge opens. I find the deeper I delve into the history of the Dunphy family, the more fascinated I become. Did you know that the castle was home to monks at one point?"

"No, I really don't know anything about the castle. Did you find anything about Catherine and Carrick in those documents?"

"Got caught up in the romance of it all, did you?"

"I did," I admitted. "Most of what I've learned about the prior residents of the castle has been pretty negative, but

Carrick and Catherine's story left me wanting to know them better. Things must have been so hard back then. I can't imagine having one baby let alone twelve in such primitive conditions."

"I imagine three hundred years from now people will look back and consider the way we live to be primitive. It's a relative term."

"I suppose you're right."

"In answer to your question, however, I did find something about them." Armand got up from the table and walked over to a bookshelf that held stacks of documents and other old paperwork.

"This is a journal written by Felicia Dunphy. Felicia was the eldest daughter of Brian Dunphy, the youngest son of the lord who ruled the castle in the late nineteenth century. It appears Felicia was educated and quite bright. She spent quite a bit of time going through both old documents and oral histories in an attempt to put together a summary of sorts for each person in her lineage. Of course the task was one that would take more than a single lifetime to complete, but the information she does provide is fascinating. I only thumbed through the journal, but I remember there was information on Carrick and Catherine. It is a very old and fragile document and I don't think it would be wise to remove it from the library, but if you would like to stay here to read it won't bother me."

"Thank you." I smiled. "I'll do that, if you really don't mind."

Armand returned to the document he had been reading when I came in and I curled up on one of the sofas with Charlie and began to read. The journal was difficult to read. For one thing, the pages were faded, and for another, there was a lot of dialect unfamiliar to me. I was able to recognize enough words on most pages to get the gist of what the writer had been trying to convey. It seemed that like me, Felicia was fascinated with Carrick and Catherine and their romance. It appeared that she'd spent quite a lot of time putting together an accounting of Catherine's life.

Catherine was the eldest daughter of an English duke. Felicia portrayed her as being very beautiful and sought by many men. It seems the duke and Carrick's father, the present lord of the castle, came to some sort of an agreement in which their eldest offspring would be married to each other. The more I read the more I began to get a clear image of a young girl who was sent by her family to marry a man she had never even met. She couldn't know at the time that he was the man she was destined to love for her entire life. How terrified she must have been on the day of her wedding.

Based on Felicia's account of the life of Catherine, it didn't appear her relationship with Carrick was one of love at first sight. In fact, there were several humorous accountings of Catherine's acts of outright defiance, which, I imagined, proved to Carrick that she had gumption, causing him to fall in love with her in the first place. It sounded like once they found each other, however, Carrick and Catherine shared a love that was both eternal and legendary.

Like Armand, I found myself wishing I had more time to spend with Felicia's journal and the other books, but Zak would most likely be wondering where I'd gotten off to and I still had a murder to solve. I reluctantly returned the book to Armand after filling him in on some of what I'd read. As a true testament to the primitive nature of the world in which Catherine and Carrick had lived, it was Catherine's fourth son who eventually inherited the title from Carrick. Catherine lost three sons in her lifetime and Carrick lost two more before he passed.

Their eldest son died when he was only five from an illness that was not identified and their fifth son, who coincidentally was named Donovan, died in childbirth. Carrick and Catherine's second eldest son was killed in battle a year before Catherine passed. Son number three as well as son number nine also died in battle prior to Carrick's demise. Based on Felicia's accounting Carrick likewise was killed in battle.

Suddenly the romance of the whole thing wasn't quite so romantic. I supposed it was common to lose children to battle and illness during the sixteen hundreds; still, I imagined to a mother, it was no less heartbreaking. I couldn't imagine losing Alex, Scooter, or Pi, and they were only borrowed children, who were destined to be part of my life only for a short time.

By the time Charlie and I headed up the stairs to our room, I found I was in a melancholy mood. Reading about the romance of ordinary lives was heartwarming and fascinating, but learning of the heartbreak contained within those same lives was something else entirely. Maybe it was preferable to read fictional accounts of lives that always ended in happily ever after.

"You okay?" Zak asked when I entered our room.

"Yeah." I sighed.

"Yeah as in not really?" Zak slipped his strong arms around me.

I rested my head against his chest. "Just thinking about the lives of those who came before us."

I explained to Zak the things I'd learned about Catherine and Carrick. Reading about the children they'd had and lost made them seem so real. I could almost imagine Catherine's impish grin as she sought to make Carrick miserable during those first defiant days of her unwelcome marriage to a man she'd never met before. I was able to experience through Felicia's retelling the magical moments that brought two souls who were destined to be together to that very conclusion prior to the birth of their first son. My heart bled with Carrick's when Catherine died, leaving him to care for an infant son and the rest of their children.

"You know," I said after Zak and I sat down on the edge of the bed, "I have to wonder why Catherine is still haunting the castle if Carrick supposedly moved on when he died in battle."

"You don't really believe all this ghost stuff, do you?"

I glared at my soon-to-be ex-husband.

"Of course you do. I'm sorry," Zak apologized. "The fact that you have a heart and a mind that's open to all things is actually one of the things I love the most about you."

Okay, so maybe he didn't have to be an ex.

"Supposing ghosts are real, how do we know that Catherine is here and Carrick isn't?"

I supposed Zak had a point. We really didn't know. Sure, Piper, Millie, and Fergus all seemed to have an opinion about which spirits moved on and which stayed, but really, all they had were opinions. At least I thought that was all they had.

"Were you able to get the satellite to work?" I wondered.

"Almost. I had to do some tweaking and build a booster, but I've almost got it. I need maybe thirty more minutes. If the storm doesn't return, we should be able to send an e-mail to the kids and anyone else you want to check in with."

"Can we Skype?"

"It's three a.m. at home."

"Oh, yeah. I keep forgetting about the time difference. You go ahead and finish what you're doing while I see if I can find Millie. I have a question for her about

Catherine. I'll be back in a half hour or so."

Thirty minutes didn't leave me a lot of time. Luckily, Millie was having tea in the arboretum. She seemed to spend almost as much time in there as Armand did in the library. Even if Lord Dunphy wasn't able to make a go of the murder mystery weekends, I was willing to bet he could get more than he did for simple lodging if he marketed things the right way.

After I sat down on the bench where Millie was sitting, I asked her about the ghosts she communicated with. I wondered if she always knew who it was she was chatting with.

"It depends. If the ghost was known to me in life, then yes, I can usually identify the energy as belonging to a specific person. If the spirit I'm communicating with wasn't someone I knew, I need a frame of reference. Most times if spirits have remained behind it's because they have unresolved issues that must be dealt with before they feel free to move on. I try to help them resolve those issues."

"Can you always see or feel the energy of the departed ones in the area?" I wondered.

"I really have no way of knowing whose energy is in range and whether I'm picking them up, but my guess is that those who seek my help reach out to me."

As much as I wanted to believe in the idea of spirits communicating from beyond, I had my doubts. Millie seemed genuine enough, but there was something that wasn't quite adding up. It all seemed too … staged.

"Is anyone here now?" I asked.

"Is there someone you're looking for?"

I wanted to ask my question about Catherine and Carrick but something stopped me. "No, just making conversation." I made a point of looking at my watch. "Gee, look at the time. I should go. I'm supposed to meet up with Zak. Have a good day."

"You too, dear. And Zoe…"

I stopped and turned. "Yeah?"

"Catherine didn't remain behind because she couldn't bear to be away from Carrick; she stayed because there was something she hid that she needed someone to find. Once that item is found she will move on to be with her love."

How did Millie know that was what I wanted to ask? The whole thing was starting to feel just a tiny bit creepy.

"Do you know what needs to be found?" I asked.

"No. It isn't for me to find. I do sense that you're connected to Catherine in a powerful way. I felt the bond the first time I met you."

"Connected? Connected how?"

Millie frowned. "I'm not sure. Are your people from Ireland?"

"The Donovans emigrated from Ireland," I confirmed.

"Interesting. Very interesting indeed." Millie looked me up and down. "Do you have children?"

"Yes. No. I mean, sort of."

Millie just looked at me.

I explained to Millie about the three minors Zak and I had living with us, as well as the school we were building for gifted youth. She asked me about my desire to have children of my own, and I found myself opening up to her about my conflicted feelings on that subject. I'm not sure why I shared so much with a woman I barely knew, but somehow I felt she would understand my internal struggle.

Millie smiled knowingly but didn't offer advice. Her supportive energy seemed to open the floodgates and I found myself discussing with her feelings I didn't even know I had. As time went on, I wondered whether Catherine had experienced all the same doubts and fears I did as she brought her first son into the world. How terrifying it must have been to love someone so much in such an unsettled and brutal time.

"I keep trying to figure out whether I'm ready. If we're ready. I wonder how a baby will affect the dynamic we have with the children who currently share our lives. I wonder how a baby will change the relationship I currently have with Zak. There are just so many unanswered questions. I know Zak wants a baby and I want to give him one, but for the life of me I can't figure out if this is the right time."

Millie took my hand in hers and gave it a squeeze. "When the time is right you will know."

Chapter 7

By the time I returned to our room Zak had managed to log on to the Internet. He warned me that the signal might only be temporary, so I typed out a quick e-mail to each of the three kids, as well as to Ellie and Levi, Jeremy Fisher, my assistant at Zoe's Zoo, and my parents. Zak sent out a few e-mails as well, and then we turned our attention to the individuals with whom we were trapped in the castle.

"I haven't figured out who Brent Silverwood is, but I'm fairly certain he isn't an actor. There's no one by that name registered with the Screen Actors Guild, and I'm coming up blank when I Google him as well."

"So if he isn't an actor why was he here?" I asked.

"I don't know. I do know that the name Dugan Westerly doesn't come up when I cross reference agents either."

I remembered Dugan Westerly was the name of the agent Lord Dunphy had said contacted him about Brent's participation in the murder mystery weekend.

"Maybe if we can figure out who Brent really was we can find out why he was killed, which might lead us to the identity of the person who killed him."

"My thoughts exactly," Zak agreed. "I'll keep looking as long as I have a signal."

"You might want to confirm the identities of the others as well. All we really have is Piper's word that any of the guests are who they claim to be, and even she admitted she'd never met some of the people who were invited."

"Okay, I'll confirm everyone's identity and then work on Brent some more if I have the time before I lose the signal. It looks like the next wave of the storm will be here in an hour or so. The good news is, now that I've boosted the signal, I should be able to log back on if it clears again."

I decided to look for Lord Dunphy while Zak worked. I found I was curious about the dungeons beneath the castle, as well as the part that had been boarded up and was no longer in use. Lord Dunphy had told me that he'd searched every inch of the castle, but the reality was that Brent Silverwood's body was missing and it had to be somewhere. If the tide had simply washed the body back onto the beach, someone would have stumbled across it by now, which led me to believe that it had to be hidden somewhere in the castle.

"Good morning, Liza," I greeted the maid who had brought me towels the previous day. She was pushing a cart with towels and toiletries, which I assumed she was delivering to the rooms that were currently occupied by guests.

"Good day to you as well, ma'am." Liza bent down to pet Charlie, who appeared to be thrilled to see her.

"I was hoping to speak to Lord Dunphy. Do you know where I might find him?"

"I'm afraid I haven't seen him since early this morning."

"Do you think he might be in his room?"

"No, ma'am. I dropped off clean linens just twenty minutes ago and his room was deserted. You might try the workroom. It seems he has been spending a lot of time down there. I imagine he is avoiding the questions he knows he will receive about the missing actor."

I noticed Liza glanced at a closed door across the hallway from where we were standing. It seemed to be an involuntary glance, almost as if she was intentionally trying not to glance at it but couldn't help herself. If I had to guess, the room she'd glanced at had belonged to Brent. I supposed it wouldn't hurt to take a look around once Liza continued down the hall.

Chances were if Brent wasn't who he claimed to be, he didn't bring any clues to his real identity with him to the castle, but there was always the possibility that even a small clue could lead us to something that would help Zak and me to figure out who he was and what he was really doing here.

"Are all the guest rooms on this floor?" I asked.

"Yes, ma'am. The guest rooms are on the second floor, Lord Dunphy occupies the third floor, and the staff is housed on the first floor, behind the kitchen."

"Do you know how long ago the part of the castle that isn't in use was sectioned off?"

"I'm sorry, ma'am, I don't know. It's been the way it is now throughout my lifetime. I believe the west wing hasn't been occupied for quite some time. Lord Dunphy should be able to answer your questions if you are able to track him down."

"Thanks. I guess I'll take a look in the workroom just in case. If you do run across him will you tell him I wish to speak to him?"

"Certainly."

I waited until Liza let herself into the next room down the hallway before slipping into the room I hoped had belonged to Brent. I didn't want to call attention to myself by knocking, so I truly hoped I wasn't going to walk in on someone in a compromising position. The doors to the guest suites locked from the inside, but as far as I could tell there was no way to lock the doors once you exited the rooms.

Luckily, the room I slipped into was dark and vacant. I turned on a lamp next to the bed and began my search. There were three suitcases in the closet. My first thought was that three suitcases were a lot for a single person on a trip that was scheduled to last only four days. Perhaps Brent's trip to Dunphy Castle was one stop on a much longer trip. The suitcases were empty, as if they'd been unpacked, but the odd thing was that based on the number of items hanging in the closet, the clothes Brent brought with him could have fit in a single case. Why the extras?

There was additional clothing in the armoire, as well as toiletries in the bathroom. I didn't find any evidence of a cell phone, wallet, passport, or other identification. It made sense that he would have had his cell phone and possibly his wallet on his person when he was shot, but his passport? A passport didn't seem like an item one would carry around on an everyday basis.

I really did wish Zak and I had taken the time to search the body for the cell phone and wallet when we'd first found it. Of course we'd had no reason to believe the body would turn up missing, so there hadn't seemed to be any urgency to check things out.

I decided to look around the room for Brent's passport. Chances were he hadn't had it on him and we really did need to find out who the man really was. If Brent was trying to hide his identity, he would have stored any identification he might have in a secure location. After all, anyone could walk in and take a look around, as I had. I looked through the drawers in the bedside table and the bathroom, although I didn't expect to find anything. I looked in the armoire, carefully removing each item of clothing, searching within the folds of the item, and then returning it to the drawer. I looked under the bed, behind the books on the small bookshelf that had been provided for the guest's enjoyment, and behind the curtains. I noticed the window in this room looked out toward the cottage where we'd found his body. Coincidence?

I stood in the center of the room and looked around. There were any number of hiding places for an item as small as a passport. I looked under the pillows on the bed, and then under the mattress. I pulled the bookshelf away from the wall and looked behind it. Nothing.

I was about to give up when I noticed that the cushion of the chair next to the fireplace looked off. I wasn't certain exactly how it was off, but it just didn't look right. I lifted the cushion and found a laptop computer. Maybe the answer to Brent's identity would be found in a document saved to the hard drive. I decided to try to sneak the computer back to our room so Zak could take a look at whatever files might be hidden on the device. The problem was that it was going to look conspicuous if someone saw me walking around with a laptop because everyone knew the Internet was down. I found a solid-colored sweatshirt in Brent's closet, which was at least three sizes too big for me, but if anyone mentioned the fact that the garment hung to my knees, I could simply say it was Zak's. I tucked the laptop up under the sweatshirt, then peeked out the door into the fortunately deserted hallway.

It was only a short distance down the hall to the room I shared with Zak. I slipped inside without anyone having seen me, or so I thought.

"That was quick," Zak commented without looking up from what he was doing.

"I decided to search Brent's room. I didn't find any ID, but I did find his laptop."

Zak turned around as I approached the desk where he was working. "Did you find his phone?"

"No, just the laptop. He probably had his phone on him when he was shot."

"True." Zak took the laptop from me, opened the lid, and turned on the power. "Just as I suspected; the machine is password protected."

"Can you get in?"

"Yeah, I can get in. It might take a while because I don't have any of my equipment and we have no way of knowing what he might have used for a password. I'll work on it when I'm done here."

"Have you found anything?" I asked.

He nodded. "I know Jessica Fielding is exactly who she claims to be, as is her niece Cassandra. Likewise, Millie Monroe really is a psychic and she actually has been credited with helping law enforcement on several missing persons cases."

"And the others?" I asked after Zak paused to read something that had loaded onto the screen.

He frowned but didn't answer.

"Did you find something?" I asked.

"It's more like what I didn't find. As far as I can tell, Sam Spalding isn't a private investigator. He doesn't seem to hold a license and I've been unable to find any information pertaining to a business under his name."

"Maybe he works illegally, without a license," I suggested.

"Maybe, but you would still think there'd be a way to look him up. How does he generate any business without an office, phone, or online listing?"

"Good question. I guess we can just ask him about his business. It wouldn't be odd to ask for a business card or phone number should we have need of his services in the future."

"It's almost time for them to serve lunch. Let's go down and see if he shows up," Zak said.

"Did you find out anything about anyone else?" I asked.

"Drew Baltimore actually is a reporter and Armand Waller really is a fairly famous historian. I haven't gotten around to checking out Susan or Luke yet. I guess we can do that after lunch, provided the Internet is still working."

As it turned out, Sam was the only one in the dining room when we arrived. After a bit of probing he admitted he wasn't really a private detective and Susan wasn't really his assistant. He told us he was an actor who had been hired to attend the murder mystery weekend playing the part of Sam Spalding, PI. He wasn't sure who had hired him because the job had been arranged through his agent. He'd never met Susan until she connected with him at the airport on the day he arrived at the castle. Zak took down the agent's name and contact information. The phone lines still weren't up, but maybe we'd be able to get off an e-mail before the Internet went down.

Piper, Jessica, and Cassandra arrived shortly after we finished speaking with "Sam," and the conversation turned to general topics such as the unwelcome return of the rain. I couldn't wait to get Zak alone so we could discuss the significance of two people who weren't who they claimed to be attending the same party. Additionally, if Sam wasn't Sam, I had to wonder who Susan really was. Unfortunately, she didn't show up for lunch. In fact, of the eleven remaining guests, the only ones who sat down for lunch were the six of us. I imagined Armand was so engrossed in his research that he'd lost track of time, and Luke might still be with Susan. Millie might have decided to take her meal in the arboretum, where she seemed to spend most of her time, and Drew could be working on her story. I really hoped Lord Dunphy would show, but Byron announced that he was otherwise occupied but would be joining us for dinner.

After we ate I decided to take Armand a sandwich. The man had to eat, and I figured it would give me an opening to discuss Luke. I knew he was Armand's teaching assistant, but it might be helpful to find out how well he knew him and how long Luke had been working with him. The more I thought about the suspects, the more I was beginning to focus on Luke. Initially, I'd believed Luke had been with Susan when Brent had been shot, but if she was sick the night of the murder, where had Luke actually been?

"I brought you lunch," I said to the professor as I set the plate with the sandwich I'd made on the table. "Roast beef left over from last night's dinner."

"Thanks," Armand said without bothering to look up.

"So how's the research going?"

"Fine."

"Did you find anything interesting?"

Armand pushed a small painting in front of me. The canvas was only about six inches by six in size. Featured on the canvas was a woman with dark hair piled high on her head wearing a blue dress. Her skin was fair and her eyes were as blue as the dress.

"She's beautiful. Who is it?"

"I believe this is Catherine Dunphy. I found the canvas tucked inside a hollowed-out book."

Armand pushed a large book across the table. Originally a book of fairy tales printed in the late eighteen hundreds, the interior pages had been carved out to provide a nesting place for the small painting.

"Why would someone hide it?" I wondered.

"I don't know. I came across it quite by accident. The book of fairy tales was shelved with some of the journals and diaries I've been looking through. I only meant to move the book so I could see what was behind it, but when I picked it up it didn't feel quite right. I opened it and found the painting."

I looked at the painting again. It really was a delicate work of art. "Why do you think this is Catherine?"

"There is a date on the back."

I turned the painting over. It was dated 1692. I remembered Lord Dunphy saying that Catherine and Carrick had lived in the castle in the late sixteen hundreds. Still, the painting could have been of anyone, and I said as much.

"While that is true, I found a letter in which Catherine's eyes were compared to the clear blue ocean on a bright summer's day. I also found a reference to her dark hair. I can't know for certain if the painting is of Catherine, but I'd say it is as good a guess as any."

I continued to study the painting as Armand ate his sandwich. The woman who'd posed for the portrait had a serene look in her eyes. I wasn't sure how anyone with as many children as she'd had could look serene, but perhaps the painting depicted an image of the woman before she'd had quite so many sons.

"This sandwich is quite good. Thank you for thinking of me. I do tend to forget to eat when I am working. When my dear

Madeline was alive she would bring me food much the way you just have. As a matter of fact, you remind me of her."

"I do?"

"She was enthusiastic and full of life, as you are. She was also intelligent and full of gumption. I imagine if she were still alive the two of you would get along just fine."

"How long has she been gone?"

"Almost five years. Some days it seems like only yesterday that she was by my side, and other times it feels as if it has been a lifetime since I have held her in my arms. Cherish what you have with your young man. Time goes by faster than you can ever imagine."

Armand seemed to enjoy his work and he appeared to be more content than most, but I could see the look of sorrow in his eyes as he stared into the distance. I couldn't imagine my life without Zak. How sad it must be to lose the other half of your soul.

"Was your wife a historian like you?"

"She was an archeologist. We never had children, but did we ever have a wonderful time traveling the globe. When she passed I found I didn't have the heart to travel the world alone so I took a teaching position."

"But you've returned to traveling?"

"To an extent. Luke came to me as an applicant for a teaching assistantship. He shared with me his desire to travel to exotic places in search of the roots of history, and I found that his enthusiasm ignited a spark in my own dark soul. We took a couple of trips together and it seemed to work out, so I resigned my position as full-time professor and we've taught part-time and traveled part-time ever since."

"I haven't seen much of Luke since we've been here."

"He tends to wander off on his own, especially if an opportunity to sample the female population presents itself. There are times I won't see him for days, but he always finds his way back."

I found it interesting that Luke and Armand traveled the world but didn't necessarily spend all their time together. I felt like that might be a significant point, but I wasn't sure if it really meant anything. Luke was obviously who he said he was. If he'd applied for a position as a teaching assistant, he must have an advanced degree in a related field. It would be easy enough to verify.

Armand had returned his attention to the document he was reading, effectively dismissing me. I picked up the empty plate and brought it back to the kitchen, then decided to check out the workroom. Several people had commented that Lord Dunphy might be holed up down there, and I remembered where the stairs were from my trip there the previous day. I thought I heard voices as I neared the entrance to the stairs, but by the time I got down it was empty. I supposed the voices could have been echoing from another location entirely, but I didn't think so. Still, I didn't see another way out of the belowground chamber and no one had passed me, so the echo from another location made sense.

When I returned to our room Zak reported that the Internet was out again, but he'd found an e-mail Alex had sent off two days ago that had somehow ended up in his spam folder. She was writing to let us know that Ellie was tied up with a project, so she and Scooter would be staying with my parents for a few days.

"What project?"

"I don't know; she didn't say."

"I hope everything is okay," I worried. "It's not like Ellie not to want to spend time with the kids. It seemed like she was really looking forward to it."

"I'm sure something came up to change her plans. The kids are fine with your parents and she knows it. Maybe there was a problem getting Brady settled in. The contractors were still there when we left, although they assured me they would be finished before Brady and his family were due to arrive. I suppose it's possible that was the issue and Ellie is tied up trying to get it straightened out."

"I suppose." It sounded like a lame excuse to me, but the reality was until we had the chance to actually speak to someone at home all the guessing in the world wasn't going to get us anywhere. In the meantime, Charlie was letting me know it was time for him to go out again. In retrospect, maybe I should have taken care of that before the storm returned.

I stood under an overhang and waited while Charlie sniffed every tree in sight before selecting one to pee on. He was happy to be outdoors even if it was raining, but personally, I wished he'd hurry up and do what he needed to do. It was cold and damp and I was tired. Having a real murder to solve had pretty much taken away the enthusiasm I'd brought to the party.

After speaking to everyone I could and gathering all the information available to us, I'd pretty much narrowed down my suspect list to Luke and Liam. Susan obviously wasn't Sam's assistant and she'd been spending a lot of time with Luke, but she'd been busy tossing her cookies while Brent, or whoever he was, was being murdered.

Luke seemed to be whom he said he was, and I supposed I had no solid reason to suspect him, but he had left the group shortly after dinner on the night Brent was killed, and he did seem to be spending a lot of time away from the rest of us and the castle. Of course Armand had as much as said Luke was known to take off for long stretches of time if a lady caught his eye, which could mean he and Susan were simply involved in a fling and therefore not interested in spending time with the rest of us.

Which left Liam: my first and it was beginning to look like my only suspect. I had no idea why he would want to kill Brent, but perhaps if Zak and I could figure out who Brent really was we'd find the motive.

"Are you almost done?" I called to Charlie.

Charlie turned and looked at me as if to ask what the rush was all about. He'd found something in a bush that seemed to interest him, so I decided to let him run around for a few more minutes. He had been pretty patient this weekend, and he had spent much more time alone in our room than he was used to.

The weekend was supposed to wrap up on Sunday and we were scheduled to fly home on Monday. I found myself wondering if that would actually happen. Not only was the bridge still closed but I imagined that once the local law enforcement found out about Brent they'd want everyone who had been present on the island at the time of his death to stick around until they could straighten things out. I wondered if Lord Dunphy had ever gotten hold of anyone about the murder. I knew he was working on a radio to do just that, but I never did hear whether he'd gotten it up and running.

I looked toward the horizon, but all I could see was rain. It certainly had been a dreary few days. I really did hope it cleared before we left. I found I was eager to take a look at the dungeons beneath the castle before we left. I couldn't imagine what it must have been like to be locked up in such a dark and dank place for days, even weeks, on end.

"Okay, Charlie, let's wrap it up," I called. "It's getting worse and I don't want to get any wetter than I already am."

Charlie barked once and then scurried into the bush he'd been playing near.

"Come on. I mean it. It's getting cold and I'd be willing to bet Zak has a nice, warm bath all ready for you and a nice, warm fire all ready for me."

Charlie scurried out from under the bush with something in his mouth. I watched as he trotted toward me, obviously proud of his find.

"What have you go there?" I asked as I bent down and took a cell phone from his mouth.

The phone was dead, so I had no way of knowing if it had belonged to Brent, but no one else on the property had mentioned losing a phone, so I was going to go out on a limb and say there was a good chance it had.

After we returned to the castle I gave Charlie a quick bath and then headed back to Brent's room to see if I could find his phone charger. Zak wasn't in the room and I wasn't certain where he'd gone off to, but he hadn't left a note so I was certain he wouldn't be gone long.

Once again I stood in the middle of the room and tried to decide where Brent might have left something like a phone charger. He'd been shot on his first night at the castle, so chances were he hadn't yet needed to charge his device. Still, I checked all the wall sockets and came up empty. I hadn't noticed it when I'd searched the drawers before, but I looked through the bedside tables anyway. Maybe one of the suitcases. I'd opened them when I was in the room the first time, seen they were empty, and then closed them. I hadn't looked for zipper pockets or other small storage areas.

I took the suitcases out of the closet one at a time and looked through all the little pockets. I didn't find anything, but I did hear a sort of bumping noise when I lifted the last case to return it to the closet. It sounded like something was rolling around in the bottom of the case, but I hadn't seen anything. I set the case back on the bed and took a second look. I ran my hands over the lining looking for any irregularity. The lining looked as if it might have been torn and then resewn in one corner. I hated to rip up the man's luggage, but he was, after all, dead. I found Brent's razor in the bathroom and used the blade to slice open the lining. What I found was something much better than a phone charger.

Chapter 8

"Who was this guy?" I asked Zak.

I'd not only found Brent's passport but I'd found four others, all with the same photo of the man we'd met as Brent but with different names and differing home countries: Brent Silverwood from Los Angeles, United States, was also Hugh Beckingham from London, Great Britain; Pierre Dupont from Paris, France; Alexander Korolova from Moscow, Russia; and Fernando Silva from Barcelona, Spain.

"I have a feeling there may be a lot more going on than we ever suspected. I think it might be time to get hold of my CIA contact." Zak's contact had helped us out on a case we'd stumbled across when we were visiting Alaska a year ago.

"How are you going to do that?" I asked. "The phones are still down and we lost the Internet."

"I checked the weather forecast before the Internet went down. We should have clearing after dark. As soon as I get a signal, I'll contact my friend and maybe we can find out what's going on. In the meantime, let's see if we can't get this phone charged. I should be able to rig something up to juice it even without the charger. I'll need some supplies. I don't suppose you know where Lord Dunphy went off to?"

"I haven't seen him."

"Okay, let's head for the workroom. Several people have mentioned that Dunphy has a bunch of tools and stuff down there. I'm sure I can find something that will work."

Once again I headed down the stairs, across the building, and toward the workroom steps, this time with Zak. You'd think with so many people staying at the castle and the weather the way it was you'd run into more people in the common rooms. I supposed that, like Armand and Millie, everyone had found a favorite spot to wait out the storm.

The workroom was deserted, which I supposed was a good thing. Zak headed over to the worktable where I'd seen his lordship tinkering with the radio that first morning. The radio was gone, but many of the tools had been left behind. I decided to look around the room while Zak searched for the things he would need.

It was a windowless room made of stone. Overhead lights had been installed, but I imagined that when the lights were off the room would exist in total darkness.

There were several worktables, as well as shelves and closets that had been pushed against the walls. The shelves held everything from power tools to canned goods.

In one corner was a wooden wall that connected to another wooden wall, which, based on the shape of the room, I assumed had been added many years later to enclose part of the overall area. The wall toward the front of the structure held a locked door. I imagined the area had been created to house the electrical system, which had been added to the castle sometime during the past century.

"It seems if there were a connection from the castle to the dungeons beneath it the passage would join with this room," I said aloud.

"Makes sense," Zak answered. "The dungeons are below the ground level of the castle, as is the workroom."

I walked slowly around the room studying the walls. If there was an entrance I'd like to find it. The idea of searching the dungeons continued to hold a certain morbid appeal.

The rest of the walls were stone and appeared to be solid. There were no visible doorways, but there were quite a few cabinets pushed up against the walls.

It made sense if Lord Dunphy didn't want people wandering around the dungeons he'd conceal the entrance from the castle, if there were indeed an entrance to conceal. I stood in the center of the room, trying to determine the general direction of the sea. The dungeons were beneath the castle and opened up to the sea, so it made sense the wall where the door to the dungeons was located would be the one at the back of the room.

I slowly walked along the wall, running my hand over the stone in search of some irregularity. There were three cabinets on this wall, all too heavy for me to move on my own, but perhaps Zak could take a minute to help me before we headed back upstairs. Based on the feel of the room it seemed that a doorway to the dungeons, if there was one, would be located in the far left-hand corner of the workroom.

"Can you help me move this?" I asked Zak.

"Did you find something?"

"Maybe."

Zak set aside the tools he had gathered and walked across the room. The cabinet was heavy, but between the two of us we managed to move it enough to determine that there was indeed a wooden door behind it. The door was padlocked, but closer examination revealed that the lock was simply hanging on a chain to which it was attached but not actually locked. We shifted the cabinet far enough away from the wall to open the doorway wide enough for me to squeeze through.

Behind the door was a dark passageway. It was much too dark to see anything at all, but there was a cool breeze coming from the depths of the inky blackness and I could hear the sound of waves crashing onto the shore in the distance. I couldn't be certain, but I was pretty sure we'd found the way to the dungeons. I returned to the workroom.

"We should come back when we have a light. And jackets," Zak added.

"Yeah," I reluctantly agreed. "Let's close this back up. If someone realizes I went through the open door they may lock it, and I really want to come back to look around."

Zak and I had just managed to return the cabinet to its original position when we heard voices from the top of the stairs.

"Hide," I whispered.

"Why?"

"Just do it."

Luckily, we were already in a dark corner of the room, where boxes and old furniture were stored, so hiding wasn't all that difficult.

"Did you leave the light on?" Lord Dunphy asked.

Darn; we'd forgotten about the light.

"Wasn't me."

I was pretty sure the person who answered was Liam, but I didn't want to peek around the stack of boxes I was hiding behind to check.

"I suppose Byron might have been down here. I really must have a talk with the chap about the cost of electricity."

"I left everything on the workbench," the second person informed Lord Dunphy.

I could hear someone sorting through the items on the workbench.

"I don't see it," Lord Dunphy said.

"I left it right there in the middle of the table," the other man answered.

"Well, it's not here now."

"Look, I get why you are doing what you are doing, but don't you think it's a bit pointless?" I was sure the voice was Liam this time.

"We are running out of time. This castle means too much to me to lose it at this point. Go find Byron and ask him if he was down here. I promised I'd show for dinner, so we'll have to wait to meet up until later this evening. I'll meet you at the cottage once I free myself up."

"Sure thing. Whatever you say."

I listened as a set of footsteps walked across the room and up the stairs. It sounded like Lord Dunphy was still in the room.

"I know the man is an idiot, but he is all I have," Lord Dunphy said.

I listened but didn't hear a reply.

"Yes, I'm sure, and no, I don't think that will work."

What will work? Who was the man talking to?

"That does seem curious. I suppose I might need to look into it further."

This one-sided conversation was both disturbing and confusing.

"I *have* been watching her and I don't know if they're connected. All we can do right now is continue with our plan."

Lord Dunphy let out a long sigh. "It's not here. Hopefully Byron has it."

I listened as Lord Dunphy walked across the room, climbed the stairs, turned off the light, and closed the door.

I was right. When the light was off the room really was totally black.

"What do we do now?" I asked.

"The stairs are about a hundred feet in front of us and maybe twenty feet to the left. There are two workbenches between us and the stairs, as well as several pieces of furniture. We'll need to move very slowly so as not to trip." Zak grabbed my hand and I held on tight. I couldn't see a thing. "Stay behind me. I'm going to inch forward."

I followed Zak as he slowly scooted his feet across the room in the general direction he'd determined the stairs to be.

"This reminds me of that time we were trapped in the mine," I commented.

"At least we don't need to worry about cave-ins this time."

Zak had a point. This time the room we were in was firmly built, but there was still something totally eerie about being immersed in complete darkness.

"What do you think Lord Dunphy and Liam are up to?" I asked.

"I have no idea. And who was his lordship talking to after Liam left? I didn't hear a second voice or a second set of footsteps."

"I think he was talking to his mother. He was speaking to her the other day as well. I'm afraid she's a bit of a nag."

"His mother? As in his dead mother?"

"Yup."

Zak stopped walking as we ran into the first workbench. We carefully made our way around it. The presence of the bench did confirm we were heading in the right direction at least.

"You don't think Lord Dunphy is somehow involved in Brent's murder, do you?" I asked.

"I don't know what to believe. The fact that Brent wasn't who he said he was brings a new aspect to the situation, and Lord Dunphy is clearly up to something. We've suspected Liam from the beginning. I suppose they could be working together. Maybe if we figure out who Brent really was and what he was really doing here we can figure out who might have wanted to kill him."

"Should we take the tools we came down for once we get the light on?" I wondered.

"Better not. Dunphy has already noticed that something seems to be missing. He might be more apt to notice additional items. I suppose the best way to handle this is to just ask him for the use of the tools upfront."

"But what if he's the killer?"

"I imagine he'll make up an excuse as to why I can't borrow the tools. I think at this point it's important for us not to draw attention to ourselves. We won't be able to snoop around freely if he starts watching us."

It took what seemed like forever for us to find our way to the stairs, but eventually we arrived there unharmed. We climbed the steps and let ourselves into the main part of the castle. There was only natural light in the room we entered, which was dim from the overcast skies, but still my eyes stung as they adjusted to the change in light.

"So what now?" I asked.

"Let's head up and get ready for dinner. We know Dunphy is going to be there. Maybe we can start up a conversation that will lead to some insight as to what everyone has been up to the past few days. It seems odd that no one ever seems to be around."

"I had that same thought exactly. It's like everyone simply disappears for the majority of the day and then random guests reappear at meal time."

Zak stopped walking. "Do you smell that?"

"Smells like food. Really good food."

"I'm starving. Hopefully whatever the cook is preparing tastes as good as it smells."

Surprisingly, everyone showed up for dinner. It was the first time everyone had shown for a meal since the first night. I don't know if there was some significance to this or if everyone had finally begun to go stir crazy on their own.

The meal was, as all the others had been, excellently prepared and presented. Tonight we were served traditional Irish dishes that had been paired with perfectly chosen wines. One thing was for certain: once I finished eating the heavy meal and sipping the excellent wine, all I was going to want to do was go to sleep. I had to wonder if that was Lord Dunphy's intent.

"This stew is absolutely to die for," Piper commented.

"It's the cook's family recipe," Lord Dunphy responded. "It's a hearty dish on its own, but be sure to leave room for the glazed corned beef. It's really quite exceptional."

The stew paired with the soda bread was a meal in and of itself. I didn't know how I was going to manage a main course, but based on the aromas coming from the kitchen I intended to try. I could diet after we returned home.

"Has there been any news on the opening of the bridge?" Jessica asked Lord Dunphy.

"I was able to contact a friend of mine on the radio. He reported that the rain should stop by midnight and the water should recede enough to open the bridge by Monday."

"That's good news. I have a book tour beginning the end of next week and I did want a chance to go home for a few days first."

"You got through to someone in town?" I clarified.

"Yes, my friend Devon."

"Did you tell him about the murder?"

"I asked Devon to inform the local law enforcement that we seemed to have a missing person," Lord Dunphy said carefully.

"Missing person? The man isn't missing; he's dead."

Lord Dunphy set his fork aside and looked directly at me. "While it is true that Mr. Silverwood has not been seen since the first night we all gathered, it is also true that other than the fact that you and your husband reported as much, there is absolutely no evidence to suggest a murder has occurred."

"Of course a murder has occurred. Why would we lie?"

"I don't know. Why would you?"

"I wouldn't. Zak wouldn't either."

"That may very well be, but so far, in spite of an exhaustive search, we have found no body, no blood, no gun, and no evidence of any type that there really was a murder. The best we can do is to file a missing person's report and hope something turns up."

The guy couldn't be serious. I looked around the table. It appeared as if the others were seriously considering Lord Dunphy's argument.

"How can he just be missing? We're on a very small island with no way off. As you already indicated, you've searched the entire area. If he's simply missing, where is he?"

"I'm afraid I don't know. I'm sure when the bridge opens everything will get straightened out."

His lordship was either in complete denial or he was lying to cover up his own part in the murder. I wanted to say more, but Zak squeezed my hand under the table as a warning not to give too much away. So far it seemed we were the only ones to take the murder seriously. I supposed it would be up to us to solve the crime; no one else seemed to be working on it. The problem was that after the bridge opened we really had no reason to stay. We were running out of time.

The rain had stopped by the time dinner was over. The clouds had parted and the stars were shining brightly. I needed to take Charlie for his evening constitutional, so Zak and I bundled up and headed out into the chilly air. It really was beautiful, with millions of tiny stars shining in the dark sky. The sea was still fairly rough, but the moon shone down onto its choppy surface, giving the night a feeling of romance.

This hadn't been the most romantic of trips in spite of the fact that the next day was Valentine's Day. I had to wonder what exactly was at work in the universe to create so many situations in which Zak and I always seemed to be caught up in one murder or another, even when we were on vacation. Was being thrown into so many murder investigations our curse or our destiny?

"Maybe we should have just stayed home," I commented. "The weekend sounded like fun, but at least in Ashton Falls we could have enjoyed our first Valentine's Day as husband and wife without all this drama."

Zak put his arm around me and pulled me against his side as we continued to walk. There was something about his strong embrace that always made me feel safe and content.

"Things didn't turn out the way I'd hoped, but in spite of the fact that pretty much everyone seems to think we made Brent's murder up, I've still had a nice time. Any time with you is perfect no matter what the situation."

"Aw, that's so sweet."

Zak kissed the top of my head. I leaned my head against his side as I watched Charlie chasing an imaginary foe. It always comforted me when Charlie was happy, and luckily he was a pretty happy little dog.

"Do you think we'll be able to get Internet when we get back to the castle?" I asked.

"Maybe. I was able to log on the last time it cleared, so I'm hopeful I can get a connection this time as well. I'm hoping to get an e-mail off to my CIA contact. I have a suspicion Brent might have been involved in something international."

"Like spying?"

"Maybe. It's hard to say, but he had something going on with all those passports. What I can't figure out is why he brought them all with him on this trip."

"There were three large suitcases in his room," I reminded Zak. "My guess is he came to the island as part of a longer trip. Maybe he was meeting someone here; maybe whoever killed him."

"I guess that's as good a theory as any. If Piper is to be believed, Lord Dunphy is hard up for money. Maybe he got himself into the middle of something he ought not to have."

"Yeah, but why invite so many people if he and Brent were meeting? It would make more sense that Brent was here to meet up with one of the other guests and Dunphy's involvement is limited to trying to downplay the murder angle in order to avoid a scandal."

"Maybe. I guess we'd have to put all the pieces together for any of it to make sense. As beautiful as this is, maybe we should head back. It's late, I'm tired, and I do want to get that e-mail off before we turn in if I can get a connection."

"Okay." I stopped walking and looked toward the field where Charlie was running around. "Charlie," I called.

He turned, looked at me, and came running as fast as his tiny legs would carry him.

"Time to head back, buddy," I said to my furry friend, who was going to need yet another bath.

"Maybe we can sneak back in and check out the dungeons tomorrow," I suggested. "I'm not sure why I'm so fascinated with them, but I am."

"I suppose there's a lot of history in those dark caverns. Dark and ugly history, but history nonetheless."

Once we returned to the room, I gave Charlie a good rinse while Zak worked on the Internet. Now that the storm had passed maybe the phone lines would come up as well. Zak seemed to think he could patch into the satellite signal if it was strong enough, and I really did want to check in with everyone at home.

I got Charlie dried off and settled him onto the rug near the fire. The poor little guy was exhausted and went directly to sleep.

"Any luck?" I asked.

"I got onto the Internet. The connection is weak, but I managed to get an e-mail off with the names we found on the passports. Hopefully my contact will be able to shed some light on who Brent Silverwood really is. The signal is too week to Skype, but you might be able to get an e-mail off to Ellie and the kids if you want."

"I want."

I sat down and hastily typed out e-mails to Ellie and each of the three children in my life. Something was up back home and I intended to find out what it was. Being unable to communicate with those you love when you know in your gut there's a problem is both frustrating and terrifying.

Chapter 9

Sunday, February 14

The following morning Zak's contact returned his e-mail with instructions for accessing a secure line. Once he'd accessed it he was able to find out that Brent Silverwood was actually an Interpol agent who had come to the island after receiving intel that a nameless, faceless person who had been selling stolen art and jewels to the highest bidder had set up a meeting with a buyer during the murder mystery weekend. The contact didn't know the identity of either the buyer or the seller.

My thoughts immediately turned to Charles Belmont. Piper had as much as admitted that Charles made his money by matching those who had something to sell with those who wanted to buy. Could he be behind whatever it was that was supposed to go down this weekend? Piper had been the one to invite the guests, and she'd already told me that both Sam and

Armand had been referred to her by Charles.

The question in my mind was why meet here in such a public place? If I had stolen art to sell, or if I was in the market for purchasing stolen art, wouldn't I simply meet the person I'd been "matched" with in a dark alley or some equally quiet place? Why come to a castle where twelve people had gathered to make the exchange? There had to be more to it. I just had to figure out what that was.

I still hadn't heard back from any of the kids, and Ellie's response to my e-mail simply had been to assure me that everything was spectacular and she hoped we were having a wonderful time. Something was definitely up. It wasn't like Ellie to be quite so vague or quite so cheery.

"So what do we do now?" I asked Zak as we dressed for breakfast.

"I'm not sure. It seems like one or both of the people involved in the illegal sale must have realized who Brent was and shot him. We need to go back over the individuals on the island and take another look at them as potential suspects. Now that we know why Brent was killed—or at least why he was involved in the weekend—we might be able to focus on someone."

"Haven't we already done that?"

"We have, but let's start again. We might very well have missed something."

"After breakfast?" I hoped. I was famished in spite of the huge meal we'd consumed the previous evening.

"After breakfast."

Surprisingly enough, almost everyone showed up for breakfast. Lord Dunphy wasn't in attendance, but everyone else was sitting at the dining table when we arrived downstairs.

"Isn't it the most divine day?" Piper commented to the group. "Sunny and relatively warm. The bridge is still closed, but the water is receding. I think it is the perfect day for a ride along the beach. Would anyone like to join me?"

"I'd like to come along," Millie answered.

"Me too," Drew added. "I might as well have a little fun because my story is going nowhere."

"I wouldn't mind a ride along the beach," Susan informed the others.

"Why don't we all go?" Jessica suggested. "We can bring a picnic and make a day of it."

"I'm afraid I have work to attend to in the library," Armand declined.

"And I really hate horses with quite a passion," Sam informed them. "I think I'll take a walk instead."

"I'll join you," Luke joined in. "I'm afraid horses are not my cup of tea, but I would enjoy some fresh air."

Everyone looked at Zak and me. We were the only ones who hadn't responded. I glanced at Zak. He winked.

"Although a ride or walk along the beach sounds enjoyable, it *is* Valentine's Day. I think my wife and I will spend the morning alone," Zak answered.

I blushed when everyone began to snicker. I knew Zak was simply buying us time to do a little sleuthing, but I couldn't help but be embarrassed when everyone looked at us with knowing glances.

"Couldn't you have just said you had a headache and wanted to stay in?" I complained to him after we went back to our room. "Everyone thinks we're…well, you know."

"We're a married couple celebrating our first Valentine's Day. What do you care what people think?"

Zak was right. Why did I care? Spending alone time with your spouse on the one day of the year devoted to romance wasn't only acceptable, it was almost expected.

"I guess you're right." I smiled. "It really is too bad we need to spend our morning redoing our suspect list."

Zak pulled me into his arms. "We may need to spend the morning sleuthing, but I can assure you, Mrs. Zimmerman, I have quite different plans for the evening."

I smiled. "You have plans?"

"I do."

I wrapped my arms around Zak's neck. "It's early. The others will be gone for hours. Maybe a preview of coming attractions?"

Zak captured my lips with his. He pulled me onto the bed and it was a very long time before we got around to that suspect list.

"Okay, read it back to me," Zak said later that morning. "At this point let's just take into account who was present at the party when Brent was killed and who wasn't. We'll look at the alibis we've uncovered and the motives we've hypothesized later."

"I guess that makes sense. As for the guests: Piper left the party early, as did Armand, Luke, and Susan. Jessica was chatting with Sam when Brent was shot and I don't remember either of them leaving. Millie was chatting with Cassandra and Drew, although Millie left to go to the ladies' room at one point. Drew left for a few minutes as well. As for the staff: Liam wasn't present in the castle at all as far as we know. Liza likewise wasn't around that evening. Lord Dunphy excused himself early. The cook was in the kitchen the entire evening, so I doubt she would have had the chance to shoot Brent. Byron moved over to act as bartender after he finished serving the meal, so I don't believe it could have been him."

"And we've already eliminated Jessica, Sam, Cassandra, the cook, and Byron, which leaves us with Piper, Armand, Luke, Susan, Millie, Drew, Liam, Lord Dunphy, and Liza as possible killers?"

"Correct."

"Who from this group had a firm and verifiable alibi?" Zak asked.

"Drew went into the kitchen for a glass of milk, which the cook verified, and Susan had the flu, which I verified the following day when I witnessed her tossing her cookies."

"Which leaves Millie, Piper, Armand, Luke, Liza, Liam, and Lord Dunphy," Zak summarized.

"Exactly."

"Who have you eliminated for reasons other than lack of opportunity?" Zak asked.

I looked down at the list in my hand. "I don't have anything concrete, but my gut tells me it wasn't Armand, Piper, Liza, or Millie. They all seem so nice, and exactly who they claim to be. I suppose that isn't a good enough reason to totally eliminate them, but if time is of the essence I'd take a hard look at Luke, Liam, and Lord Dunphy. Initially I didn't think Dunphy had a motive, but after what we heard in the workroom I'm not so sure."

"Almost everyone is away from the castle today. How about we take a look in the rooms of the guests we can't definitively eliminate? I'll take Armand and Luke and you take Piper and Millie. We'll meet back here when we're done."

It was a good idea not to eliminate anyone based on a gut feeling alone, but I did feel a little odd searching Millie and Piper's rooms. They were right next door to each other, making it easy to take a peek in each room without the need to spend too much time in the hall, where one of the staff might see me lurking around.

Piper's room was almost twice as large as Zak and mine, although ours was plenty big. I supposed Lord Dunphy had let Piper select her room because she was helping him with the project. Initially I wouldn't have imagined the sweet and slightly wacky woman Zak and I had met on our honeymoon could ever be a killer, but it was nagging me that she had been behind the invites, including, most likely, of both the seller and the buyer Brent had attended the event to find. Could Charles's matchmaking extend to the black market, and was Piper part of the operation or simply a clueless pawn?

My initial investigation didn't find anything odd. Empty suitcases under the bed, clothing in the dresser and closet, one of Jessica's books next to the bed, toiletries in the bathroom. There was absolutely nothing to suggest that Piper was up to anything other than vacationing. There was a notepad next to the phone, which hadn't been working since the first day we'd been there. The top sheet of paper on the notepad was blank, but I put the whole thing in the pocket of my sweatshirt anyway. When I got back to my room I'd take a closer look at all the pages to see if anything was written on a page toward the middle, which is what I would have done if I'd been trying to hide a message.

I sifted through the drawer located in the table at the side of the bed. Piper's passport was in the drawer. I opened it to find a book full of stamps, the most recent of which were for trips to Barcelona, Paris, and Moscow. I had to wonder if it was a coincidence that those were cities where three of Brent's fake passports claimed he lived. Of course all three were major cities and Piper had never made a secret of the fact that she traveled widely and often.

I jotted down the dates just in case.

I really didn't see anything out of place, so I decided to head next door to Millie's room. The first thing I noticed when I walked in was an envelope on the bed with my name written on it next to a small flashlight. I opened the envelope and pulled out two pieces of paper.

Dear Zoe,

> *My intuition told me you'd be by this morning. Not to worry; I am not upset that you needed to take a second look. I know you know that I did not kill Brent, but I also know there are times when you let your mind question what you know in your heart to be true.*

I have included in this envelope my journal entry from the day we all arrived. I believe it may help you to sort things out.

Oh, and take the flashlight I left on the bed when you leave. You will need it.

Hugs, Millie

I slipped the flashlight into my pocket and looked at the second sheet of paper. It had been torn along one side, as if she had literally ripped it from her journal.

February 11

Such an interesting group we have assembled here at the castle. I can feel the energy change just a bit as each new guest arrives. I thought this might be a boring weekend, but I can see that I am in for a rollicking good time. Piper and I were the first to arrive, followed by Jessica Fielding and her niece, Cassandra. Piper is positively glowing with excitement as she meets her favorite author for the first time.

Professor Armand Waller and his guest, Luke, arrived next. Armand has already drifted away mentally as he ponders the significance of each and every artifact within these ancient walls, but I can see that his friend Luke bears a secret. A dark secret that provides a harshness to the otherwise cheerful mood.

I already knew Luke was somehow wrapped up in this whole thing; now I just needed to figure out how exactly. I continued to read.

Sam Spalding and Susan Langtree are the next to arrive. Neither are who they claim to be. Sam's energy is all wrong for the role he professes to play. I believe that in time his truth will be revealed. He seems harmless enough; I just wish I could say the same thing about Susan. Her energy is dark and unsettled. All is not well.

I supposed the "dark and unsettled" energy Millie was picking up on could have been the illness that would inflict itself upon the woman claiming to be Susan Langtree later that day.

Drew Baltimore has an aggressive energy that at the moment seems to be passive, bordering on melancholy. She is smiling, but her smile does not reflect her inner state. I do not sense a specific threat from her, but I also sense a restless energy that is demanding to be satisfied.

I am most worried about the man who calls himself Brent. He is not at all who he appears to be. He professes to live in the spotlight, but I can see he lives in the shadows. I sense a darkness surrounding him, although unlike Luke and Susan, whose energy is dark from within, I feel an external darkness surrounding Brent.

It was almost as if Millie knew how things would play out. I wondered if she'd tried to warn Brent about this external threat. I also wondered if he would have listened to her had she tried.

> And last but not least, we have the charming Zoe Donovan and her handsome husband. Zak is exactly who he professes to be: a man with a pure and giving heart who is deeply in love with a woman he can't seem to keep his eyes off of. Zoe, however... Perhaps it is not my place to say.

"Say what?" I said aloud, to no one in particular. I looked in the envelope for another journal page, but there was nothing there. I had an overwhelming urge to tear the place apart, looking for the book the entry had originally been recorded in, but deep inside I knew there was nothing more to find. One thing was for sure: I was going to ask Millie what she meant before we left the island.

I was about to head back to our room to meet with Zak, but at the last minute I decided to check out Susan's room. I had eliminated her from the suspect list because she'd said she was sick on Thursday evening and I'd witnessed her vomiting on Friday, but I kept thinking that Millie had said her energy was dark and unsettled.

I hoped everyone would be away as long as I had originally estimated; I really didn't want to get caught snooping in other people's rooms.

Susan's room was much like the others, although not nearly as neat as Piper and Millie's. I looked around but didn't see anything unusual on the surface. I quickly opened drawers and closets, finding nothing out of the ordinary. I took a cursory look around the bathroom and found something that changed everything.

I quickly slipped out the door and into the hall. Boy, did I have news for Zak. I was heading back to our room when I heard my name. Or at least I thought I did. The sound was really faint, and in all honestly it could have been the wind whistling through the old structure, but it was enough to cause me to look around.

When I'm asked about this later, I'll confess that I really wasn't sure what I saw, but in that moment I was certain Catherine Dunphy was standing at the end of the hallway, beckoning me to follow her. I'm not certain why I did. Deep inside, I knew it must be an illusion that faded from sight as quickly as it appeared. I knew Zak was waiting for me and would be worried if I was delayed, but I found myself walking to the spot where the image had been standing.

I'd thought a lot about what Millie had said about Catherine and me being linked in some way. I'm not sure how that could be possible, but I believe that it's true. I know I'd thought about her quite a bit ever since I'd been at the castle. I'd thought about the love she had for her husband and the twelve sons she bore him.

When I got to the end of the hallway I tried to decide if I should turn left or right. Neither direction seemed better than the other until I noticed a faint light in the distance of the left-hand corridor. I turned in that direction and slowly made my way past closed doors that were beyond the area used by the current castle guests or staff. When I got to the end there was a door. The dust on the floor in front of the door, in addition to the rusted handle, evidenced the fact that the door hadn't been opened in years. I didn't expect the door to open suddenly, but I'd come this far so I reached out and gave the handle a twist. It turned easily.

When I opened the door I was greeted by a cold draft. Unlike the hallway I had come from, the corridor I entered had no power and, apparently, no heat. I realized I had entered an older part of the castle that probably hadn't been inhabited for at least a century. I took out my flashlight and made my way down the dark hall. I had no idea if I should continue on or perhaps enter one of the hallways intersecting the one on which I was walking. If I'd thought the castle was huge before, I now realized how enormous it really was.

"Okay, now where?" I asked out loud, considering all the routes available to me. If Catherine wanted me to follow her, she was going to have to make an appearance or I was heading back to the warmer and much cheerier side of the door. I hadn't planned to leave the warmth of the castle, so I only had on a sweatshirt, not a jacket.

I waited in silence. I know this is crazy, but I swear I could hear the castle breathing. The flashlight I carried only penetrated the darkness so far before the glow it provided was swallowed up in the void.

I don't remember seeing or hearing anything, but I do recall having the feeling that I should keep moving onward. When I came to a fork I sensed I should take the right-hand passage, just like I knew the door at the end would lead to stairs that would take me downward. I walked slowly along the stairway. It was narrow and made of stone, and there were no windows or exit points. I had to fight a feeling of claustrophobia as I made my way deeper and deeper into the inky darkness.

I'm not sure how far I traveled—over two, maybe three stories—before I came to a door at the bottom of the stairs. Just as the door above it had looked like it hadn't been opened in decades, it also gave way easily. The door opened into a windowless room that was completely empty. I stepped into the center of the room and looked around. This circular room was made of stone, with no windows or other exits. I had no idea why Catherine would have led me to this extremely isolated yet completely empty space.

"I don't understand what you want from me," I said into the void.

I listened for an answer. I was sure I heard voices, but they seemed to fade as soon as they sounded. I imagined sound must carry in the old castle. In all reality I could be hearing voices echoing from other parts of the building. I slowly turned in a complete circle, trying to figure out what to do next.

The strange thing about the empty room is that it should have felt hollow, barren, devoid of life and energy. But somehow it didn't. Somehow the longer I stood in the center of the round room the warmer I became. I could almost imagine the echo of music and laughter. I felt as if the room contained memories of years gone by, when the now empty room was alive with the people who had lived in the castle all those years ago.

I closed my eyes as I tried to imagine what this isolated room could have been used for. It seemed to exist alone at the bottom of the stairs, but perhaps at one time it was part of a passage to other rooms inhabited by Dunphy ancestors.

I'm not sure what caused me to walk forward, to push against the specific stone I did. It looked no different from any of the others. I guess I decided to let my heart lead my head, and my heart was telling me that Catherine had brought me here for a reason.

I stood back as a section of the wall gave way to a much smaller room filled with what looked to be personal treasures. There were treasures from childhood such as wood-carved toys, clothing to fit a toddler, and a tiny infant's cradle with a blanket inside that said *Amelia*. There were treasures from adulthood such as a special dress, a woven rug, pottery, and hand-crafted furniture. I slowly made my way into the room, being careful not to touch anything that might be damaged by my touch all these years after it was created. I'd obviously found someone's secret place. I'd had such a place in an old cave behind my house when I was a kid. It was a place for me to keep my treasures. A place for me to spend time alone when the world became too much for me to handle.

I walked over and sat down on a chair. I tried to imagine Catherine with her twelve sons sitting in this very spot. It must have been a hard life even for the privileged. I didn't blame her a bit for wanting a place of her own to escape to.

I looked at the cradle. The name on the blanket was clearly that of an infant daughter. Catherine had borne only sons. Perhaps this wasn't Catherine's secret spot after all.

I closed my eyes and leaned back into the chair. I could so clearly imagine Catherine sitting in the chair, singing to her babies. On the surface she appeared content and serene, but I know that in addition to the love she felt for her family, her heart was filled with fear and sorrow. The emotions I imagined were so raw and intense that I opened my eyes in order to fend off the pain.

I looked around the small yet cozy room. I imagined that every item must hold great significance to the one who'd placed it there. Next to the chair was a box. I opened it and gasped.

"I see you found my treasure," a voice said from behind me.

Chapter 10

When I became conscious my first thought was of the pounding in my head, followed by the cold hardness of the floor beneath my body. It took me a few minutes to remember what had happened. It was completely dark. So dark that I couldn't even see the hand I held up to my face. I was cold. So very, very cold. The floor beneath me was made of stone.

I couldn't remember how I came to be here in this dark chamber, but the dampness on my forehead, coupled with the throbbing in my temple, seemed to indicate that I'd suffered a blow to the head. I tried to sit up but found the movement made me dizzy, so I lay back down until the dizziness passed.

Once I was able to sit up I looked around, but the movement did me no good because there was nothing to see. I tried to remember what had happened in the minutes before I woke up here. I remembered walking through the castle. I was following someone. Catherine.

I remembered walking down an endless flight of stairs. The hollow darkness seemed to envelop me, as if I were traveling through a void separating time and space.

I remembered the circular room and the feeling of light, warmth, and belonging that seemed to fill my soul as time passed. The emptiness in my heart was enough to let me know that I was no longer in that special room. The question was, where was I now?

It was cold and dark and I could hear the sound of the ocean in the background. I had the sense that I wasn't being held within the castle walls. The only conclusion left to me was that I'd been left in the dungeons beneath the castle. I rolled over onto my knees and then slowly stood. I reached out my arms, which met with nothing but empty space. I had no idea which direction would lead to the light and which would take me further into darkness.

I sat back down on the floor as I tried to figure out what to do. I knew that by now Zak would be looking for me, my knight in shining armor who always saved the day. He'd want me to wait for him, so I would wait.

I crossed my legs and tried to curl my body into itself for additional warmth. Waiting wouldn't be easy in this dark and frigid place, but at the moment I didn't see that I had all that many options. I needed a distraction, so I used my time to try to figure everything out.

When I'd gone into Susan's bathroom I'd seen she had a bottle of ipecac. Ipecac is used to induce vomiting, and I realized that her little demonstration on Friday was simply to provide herself with an alibi for Thursday. I don't think she necessarily planned to use an illness as an alibi; it occurred to me that she was a bulimic who carried the stuff with her wherever she went, and my stopping by her room provided the situation she needed.

The question remained, had Susan killed Brent, and if she was involved in the buy/sell operation, was she the buyer or the seller?

And then there was Lord Dunphy. His was the voice behind me but it hadn't been Dunphy who had hit me. I'd turned to speak to the lord of the castle, who I guess technically owned the jewels. We'd both had our backs to the door when someone came in from the staircase and hit me. I remembered the look of surprise on Dunphy's face before I blacked out. He may or may not have been part of a scheme to buy and sell something, but I didn't think he'd followed me to the room with the intention of hurting me. I think he somehow knew that, for whatever reason, Catherine would lead me to the jewels that had been hidden all these years.

Zak had said Brent had come to the island to catch an international thief. I really doubted Dunphy was that person, and I also doubted he was the buyer. Which meant that there were two other people involved. I suspected Susan was one of the two, with maybe Luke or Liam? I might not have all the answers, but as soon as I got out of there I planned to resolve any unanswered questions that remained.

I was attempting to focus on my breathing so as to avoid hysteria when I heard a sound to my right that sounded like groaning.

"Is someone there?"

The groaning grew louder.

"Lord Dunphy?"

"Ms. Donovan? Is that you?"

"It's me. Are you okay?"

I waited in silence for a response. It seemed as if an eternity passed before the person next to me responded that he was very much *not* okay.

"Did you see who hit me?" I asked.

My question was met with silence.

"Lord Dunphy? Are you still with me?"

I scooted across the stone floor in the direction from which I'd heard his voice when there was no response. I just hoped I'd find Dunphy still alive. I'd been hit on the head, and while it smarted, I didn't think it was terminal, but I had no idea what had been done to his lordship. For all I knew, he could have been shot.

I paused several times during my journey across the floor to gauge the accuracy of my direction. I couldn't see a thing, but if I listened closely enough I could hear the slight sound of breathing. Maybe Dunphy knew a way out of here. Of course I was going to have to figure out a way to wake him up long enough to get him to tell me what that way might be.

It took quite a bit longer than I had anticipated, but eventually my outstretched hand met with flesh and blood.

"Lord Dunphy," I tried, gently shaking his shoulder. It was obvious he was passed out cold. I could feel a dampness on his shirt, probably blood. "Can you hear me?"

Dunphy groaned.

"We need to get out of here. It feels like you've lost a lot of blood. Any idea where we are or how to get back to the castle?"

"Dungeon."

"I sort of figured that. I'm not familiar with the layout. Do you think we're in a cell?"

Lord Dunphy groaned again, but I felt him sit up beside me. Maybe he wasn't hurt as badly as I'd thought.

"The cells no longer lock. Unless Luke fashioned a locking device of some sort we should be able to get out of here. Eventually."

"So it *was* Luke. He was number two on my suspect list, behind Liam."

"Suspect list?"

"I ranked the other guests based on the likelihood that they'd killed Brent, who isn't really Brent, by the way."

"Brent isn't Brent?"

"I'll explain later. How do you suggest we find our way out of here?"

"The floor slopes gently toward the ocean. If you travel down the slope you will reach the entrance on the beach. If you travel up the slope you'll find the entrance in the workroom."

I felt the floor near where I was sitting. Dunphy was correct; the ground sloped enough to actually determine a direction. If you were heading toward neither the beach nor the workroom you would be traveling parallel to the entrances.

"Okay, what do you suggest? Up or down?"

"Down, I think. Unless someone has moved the cabinet in front of the door in the workroom we will be trapped at that point."

I touched Dunphy's shoulder with my hand. "Can you move?"

He let out a deep sigh, or maybe it was another groan. "I can move. I assure you that I have no intention of dying in my own dungeons."

Dunphy and I began to crawl toward the downward slope. It was slow going, but crawling seemed to make the most sense when there was no way to see where we were stepping.

"I guess Luke got the jewels?"

"Blackguard. Those are my jewels. I've been looking for them for most of my life."

"So you never found the hidden room?"

"The door leading to the stairway has always been frozen shut. It is a heavy door. Built to last an invasion. I've never been able to open it."

"But it opened right up." I stopped crawling when I felt something rough on the ground. Whatever it was, it was sharp enough to cut right through human skin. I warned Dunphy and we scooted our way around it.

"For you. Mother said you were the one."

"The one?" I asked.

"The one Catherine has been waiting for. I knew it was only a matter of time before Catherine revealed her secret to you, so I have been watching you. I followed you today. At least I think it is still today. It's hard to tell."

"I'm pretty sure we haven't been down here for more than an hour or two at the most. Zak would have found me by now if it had been longer."

"You seem pretty confident of your young man."

"I am," I answered, and I was. Still, it seemed like Zak should have come looking for me in the dungeons by now. He'd know I was missing and he knew I was fascinated by them. I hoped he was okay.

I stopped crawling when my hand came into contact with metal bars. "I think we're at the edge of the cell."

"You will need to find the door. As I said, unless Luke fashioned a lock it should open to the main walkway."

I stood up. The bars gave me a frame of reference and something to hold on to. "I'll go left and you go right. Whoever finds the opening first should holler."

It took a few minutes, but eventually I found the doorway that led into the cell. Not only was it not locked, it wasn't even closed. Luke must not have been too worried that we would regain consciousness.

Once we made our way to the walkway that ran down the center of the old cells, it was just a matter of maintaining our downward journey. As we neared the opening from the beach to the dungeons it began to get lighter. Eventually, it was light enough for us to see where we were going.

Dunphy was in pretty bad shape. I was surprised he'd made it as far as he had. I instructed him to stay put while I went for help. There was no way he was walking back into the castle with a bullet in his chest.

I snuck in through the door behind the kitchen. I figured Luke would have to wait around until the bridge opened, and he might be using force to ensure that the others didn't come looking for me. I was right. I looked out from the kitchen into the dining room. All the other guests, as well as the staff except for Liam, were sitting around the table. It looked as if their hands were tied behind their backs. Luke stood at one end with a gun in one hand and Charlie in the other. I guess that explained why Zak hadn't come looking for me.

What I found interesting was that Susan was sitting at the table with the others. I'd really thought she was in on the whole thing.

Now I just had to figure out how to save everyone so that everyone could save Lord Dunphy.

I stepped back into the kitchen as I assessed the situation. Luke had a gun. I didn't. There were knives in the kitchen, but everyone knows guns trump knives. Additionally, Luke had my fur baby in his arms. There was no way I was going to do anything that might lead to Charlie being injured. It seemed a direct invasion of the room wasn't going to lead to anything good.

What I needed was a diversion. I needed to be careful, though, because I didn't want to make things worse. Still, Dunphy was in bad shape, so I had to act quickly. I had an idea. Granted, it was a lame idea, but it was all I had. I was about to put my lame idea into action when someone clamped a hand over my mouth from behind.

"Don't scream," a voice I recognized as Liam's said in my ear.

I stood perfectly still. I *knew* Liam was part of this. I should have trusted my first instinct. Of course if he was working with Luke, why was he lurking around in the kitchen with me?

"If I remove my hand will you remain silent?"

I nodded my head that I would. I really had nothing to gain by drawing Luke's attention to our presence.

Liam slowly removed his hand. I took a deep breath and turned around so that we were facing each other. "Are you working with Luke?" I whispered.

"Does it look like I'm working with Luke?"

"No," I admitted, "I guess not."

"I need you to go back outside and circle around to the front of the castle. Once you get there create a disturbance. Can you do that?"

"Yeah," I assured him. "I can do that."

I let myself out the back door, circled around to the front, then opened the front door and stepped inside yelling, "Honey, I'm home," as loudly as I could.

Luke stepped toward my voice while Liam came in behind him and hit him over the head with something. The blow didn't kill him, but it did knock him out.

After Luke's gun had been removed from his possession and he'd been secured, the men went to rescue poor Lord Dunphy. Luckily, his wound looked worse than it actually was and it appeared he would make a full recovery.

About the time Lord Dunphy was settled in his rooms, the phones came back on line and Zak was able to get hold of both a doctor and the local authorities.

Once law enforcement arrived and everything got sorted out, it was discovered that Luke had taken the job with Armand in order to travel the world, with access to restricted locations under the radar. All those times Armand thought Luke was partying it up with the woman of the moment, he was actually procuring priceless jewels, artifacts, and works of art, which he'd later sell to the highest bidder. On this particular trip he was here to sell a diamond worth close to a hundred million dollars to Susan, who had come as the representative of her very rich and very extravagant boss. She needed a cover so she hired Sam to be her pretend boss. Once Luke and Susan heard about the jewels Catherine had supposedly hidden in the castle, they'd decided to look for them. After all, the bridge was closed, so they weren't going anywhere.

Neither Luke nor Susan admitted to killing Brent. It seemed a foregone conclusion that they were lying, but something about their story seemed to ring true. They both stated that they'd simply met in Luke's room for the exchange. After the police had finished with her, I asked Susan why she'd made up the flu thing if she hadn't killed Brent, and she said that once she heard about Brent's death she'd realized she would need an alibi to avoid closer scrutiny. She saw her opening at dinner and took it.

All in all, this murder mystery weekend had been a lot more exciting than I could ever have imagined.

By the time evening rolled around Luke had been arrested, Lord Dunphy had been taken to the local medical facility, and the rest of us had settled in for our last evening together. Because the original weekend wasn't supposed to wrap up until Sunday at dinner, no one had flights until the next day.

I suggested to the other guests that we invite the staff to dine with us and they agreed. After everyone except Liam gathered around the table, Zak toasted our health and we all dug into the delicious meal the cook had prepared.

"Do you think we should go out to the stable and invite Liam in?" I wondered.

"There's no need," Zak answered. "Liam left after the local law enforcement wrapped things up."

"Left? Where did he go?"

"He didn't say."

I guess it wasn't all that odd that one of the castle staff would take advantage of some time off and head to the pub, but I never had gotten the chance to thank him for what he'd done to help me diffuse a potentially tragic situation.

Although I'd only known this group of people for four days, I felt that I was really going to miss a few of them. Maybe I'd ask for addresses and try to stay in touch.

Zak's phone dinged. He looked at the caller ID. "I'm sorry; I really have to take this."

It was unlike Zak to bring his phone to the table, especially when we were out, so the only thing I could gather from his behavior was that he had an important call that he'd been expecting. After he completed his call he excused himself and headed upstairs.

"Excuse me," I said to the group. "I think I need to find out what's going on. Zak isn't usually one to put work over time with friends."

"Of course, dear," Piper answered for the group. "I do hope everything is all right."

I smiled at Piper and then ran up the stairs to our room. Zak was on the phone again, but he motioned for me to come in and close the door.

"What's going on?" I asked.

"That was my CIA contact. I had a hunch and forwarded Liam's photo to him before he left."

"Hunch? What hunch? Liam saved our lives. He turned out to be the good guy, remember?"

"He is the good guy; he's just not who you think he is. As it turns out, Liam was responsible for having Brent's body moved."

I frowned. "Why would he do that?"

"Because Liam is also Interpol. He was here as Brent's partner. When we told him that Brent was dead he cleaned it up. He figured he couldn't afford to have Brent's real identity discovered."

Okay, I had to admit this was a twist, but I supposed it made sense. The main reason I'd suspected Liam was because he was able to move around so freely; he was the one we happened to first report the death to and he was the one Lord Dunphy had sent to check on the body. It would be easy enough for him to move the body before anyone other than Zak and I even knew Brent was dead.

"There's still one unanswered question: Who killed Brent? Both Luke and Susan swear it wasn't either of them."

"There is one possibility we never really considered."

"Who?"

"If we go back to our original list we find that Piper left the party early, as did Armand, Luke, and Susan. Jessica was chatting with Sam, and Millie was chatting with Cassandra and Drew. Millie left to go to the ladies' room at one point. Drew left for a few minutes too, but we know she was in the kitchen. As for the staff, Liam and Liza weren't around that evening. The cook was in the kitchen the entire evening and Byron moved over to the bar after he finished serving the meal. And Lord Dunphy excused himself early."

"We've already been through this multiple times," I complained.

"I know, but bear with me. I have a point."

"Okay, go ahead.

"That leaves us with Piper, Armand, Luke, Susan, Millie, Drew, Liam, Lord Dunphy, and Liza as having opportunity. If Liam is Interpol and we believe Susan and Luke that they didn't kill Brent, that leaves Piper, Armand, Millie, Liza, and Lord Dunphy."

"Are you saying one of those five people killed Brent?"

"I believe so."

I frowned. "Which one?"

"I believe it was Liza. The local police are picking her up now."

"Liza? Why would Liza kill Brent?"

Zak pulled up a photo on his phone and showed it to me. In it, the man we knew as Brent was standing over the body of a man who looked to be dead. It appeared he had been shot in the back.

"Liza is connected to the dead man?"

"He was her brother."

"Her brother the soldier?"

"I guess you could say that. My contact at the CIA informed me that Liza's brother was a member of a still-active splinter group of the IRA. He was killed during a standoff five years ago. Brent, whose name is really Gregory Kline, was charged with shooting him during a demonstration. The incident was reviewed, and it was determined Brent had acted according to protocol."

"So Liza sees a chance to get her revenge. What are the odds that the man who killed her brother would show up at the castle where she cleans rooms?"

"Pretty astronomical."

"How did she even know who he was?" I wondered.

"Apparently this photo was all over the news and the Internet at the time of the event. I imagine she's been studying that photo for five years. Other than changing his clothes Gregory did nothing to disguise himself. Anyone familiar with the photo would have recognized him."

I felt a sadness wash over me. Liza was such a sweet person. I couldn't imagine her shooting anyone. Still, if her brother's death had been a festering wound all these years. I suppose I could see how it might set her off to find one of the guests at the castle was the man who had destroyed not only her brother's life but the lives of herself and her mother. How incredibly sad that all these years later a senseless act of violence could still destroy lives.

"What do you think will happen to her?"

"I don't know," Zak answered. "I guess that's up to Interpol to sort out, if my theory is indeed correct."

Chapter 11

My last night at the castle turned out to be a sleepless one. The thought of poor Liza wasting her life in jail depressed me more than I was able to deal with. After Zak fell asleep I slipped on my robe and headed down the stairs. Maybe some warm milk would help me sleep. When I entered the kitchen I found Millie sitting at the table sipping a cup of tea.

"Couldn't sleep either?" I asked.

"Restless spirits."

"I see. Who's out and about tonight?"

"Catherine, and she seems quite vexed."

I frowned. "I found the jewels. They've been returned to Lord Dunphy. I would think she would have moved on. Didn't you say the reason she hadn't moved on was because there was something she needed someone to find?"

"I did say that, but it seems the jewels were not what she wanted you to find."

I poured myself a glass of milk and then sat down next to Millie. "Okay, if it wasn't the jewels keeping her here, what was it?"

Millie sighed. "I'm afraid I don't know."

I took a sip of my milk and pondered the situation. "She led me to her secret room," I began. "Whatever it is she wants me to find must be in the room. I was waylaid when the jewels were found and first Lord Dunphy and then Luke showed up. Perhaps I should go back."

"I think that would be a good idea. Whatever Catherine's secret is, I am convinced that you are to be the one to uncover it. Your energy is linked to hers in a very definitive manner."

I had to admit I could feel Catherine's presence as I sat talking to Millie. She seemed anxious, almost desperate. I was leaving the following day. I supposed if I was to fulfill the act I seemed destined for, it would have to be tonight.

"Would you like to come with me?" I asked Millie.

She looked to a spot over my head and smiled. "Yes. Catherine is fine with my coming along. We should go now, before it gets any later."

I retraced the steps I'd taken the previous afternoon. Down the narrow hallways and even narrower stairs. As on the day before, the old part of the castle was drafty and more than just a little bit cold. When we got to the round room I pressed the stone to reveal the secret room. Millie gasped as I stepped inside.

"This is so familiar," Millie whispered. "I feel as though I've been here before."

I stood in the middle of the room and looked around. I had no idea where to start looking for whatever it was Catherine wanted me to find. My eyes settled on the cradle. "Do you know who Amelia was?"

Millie closed her eyes, as if focusing on my question. I knew Catherine had twelve sons. Perhaps Amelia was a sister?

Millie held her hand to her chest.

"What is it?" I asked.

"I feel such a deep sorrow. It is almost overwhelming. Oh, God."

I watched as a tear slid down Millie's cheek.

"The cradle," Millie said. "The secret is in the cradle."

I bent down and looked inside the cradle. Other than the blanket with the name Amelia on it, it appeared to be empty. It was made of wood, with a solid bottom. I ran my hand over the wood. Perhaps what had once been in the cradle was long gone. But wouldn't Catherine know that?

"I don't see anything."

"Look beneath the surface."

Beneath the surface? The room we were standing in was hidden by a secret door; perhaps the cradle had a secret door as well. I ran my hand over the wood again. I felt a slight catch in one corner. I gently pressed the corner and the bottom gave way to another wooden bottom beneath the first. Between the two layers was a very old piece of parchment with writing on it.

"It looks like a letter," I informed Millie.

"Can you read it?"

"It's so old. I hate to touch it for fear of destroying it."

Millie was silent for a moment. "Catherine wants you to try."

I gently lifted out the centuries' old message and began to read. Like the journal I'd read earlier in the weekend, the words were faded and difficult to make out.

"It says something about having a daughter," I began. I squinted to make out the next part. "She was born while her husband was away in battle."

"She had a child out of wedlock?" Millie asked.

I tried to make out the next part of the passage. There were words I didn't understand, making it even more difficult to read. "I don't think so. I think Amelia was conceived before Carrick left for battle but delivered while he was away." I frowned as I tried to continue. "Catherine believed Garrick would not welcome a female child. She is frightened for her fate when he returns."

I bit my lip as I tried to make out the rest of the letter. "She wants Amelia to be raised in a family where female children as well as male offspring are cherished and loved. She believes Carrick will dismiss her in favor of her brothers. She believes he will marry her off for political reasons as soon as she is old enough. He sounds like a monster."

Millie closed her eyes and gently rocked back and forth. "No, I don't sense that Catherine thought of her husband as a monster. I sense sadness in her heart, but she loves her husband in spite of his quite chauvinistic view of women. It is not anger at her husband that I am picking up but rather love for her daughter, and the yearning that she will be given opportunities most women back then didn't have. She wants her to be something other than a pawn."

I continued to decipher the letter one word at a time. "There is a family she knows. A family she feels will give Amelia the love she would most likely not receive as a female child of Carrick's."

"She gave her daughter away," I realized.

I watched as Millie gasped.

"It is true," Millie confirmed. "I can feel it in my soul. Poor Catherine. Her heart was breaking as she wrote this. What a difficult decision."

I took Millie's hand in mine as I tried to make sense of the whole thing. Wouldn't her husband notice if he came home from battle and his wife was no longer pregnant but there was also no baby?

"The baby she lost. Son number five. Donovan. She didn't lose a child in childbirth; she had a daughter," I realized.

Millie squeezed my hand in support. "Yes, I believe that makes sense."

I handed Millie the parchment. There was more to read, but I found I'd lost the heart for it. "I guess I understand *why* she did it. What I don't understand is *how* she could do it. To give away your own flesh and blood?"

"Love trumps all."

I guess Millie had a point. What wouldn't I do for Alex, and she wasn't even my flesh and blood. I guess when you decide to love a child you decide to put the needs of that child ahead of all else, even your own happiness. I had to wonder why it was so important to Catherine for me to find this. She'd basically stayed behind so she could lead me to this secret hundreds of years after Amelia had died. If she wanted someone to find out about Amelia it seemed she could have found someone else within the past three hundred years. Why me and why now?

"Oh, my," Millie said as I stared down at the empty cradle.

"What is it?"

"Look at the name of the couple Catherine gave Amelia away to."

She handed me back the parchment and pointed to a line toward the bottom of the page. The ink was faded, but it clearly said Amelia would be raised by Conall and Deirdre Donovan.

Zimmerman Academy

The New Normal

By Kathi Daley

Ellie has been holding down the fort while Zoe and Zak have been away. Find out what she's been up to in *The New Normal*: Book 1 in the new Zimmerman Academy short story series.

Recipes for *Shamrock Shenanigans*

Reuben Dip—submitted by Nancy Farris
Mexican Potatoes—submitted by Janel Flynn
Pot Roast with Dumplings—submitted by Della Williamson
Corn Casserole—submitted by Pam Curran
Peanut Butter Brownie Cake—submitted by Teri Fish
Triple Layer Pistachio Pie—submitted by Vivian Shane

Reuben Dip

Submitted by Nancy Farris

This recipe is my go-to for potlucks at work. I just put everything in the Crock-Pot when I leave home, then plug it in and heat it up for about an hour when I get to work. There is never a drop of it left.

4 oz. deli corned beef, trimmed and chopped finely
8 oz. cream cheese, cubed
8 oz. sour cream
8 oz. Swiss cheese, cubed
1 cup (8 oz.) sauerkraut, drained and rinsed
¼ cup Thousand Island dressing

Serve with rye bread or rye crisp crackers.

Mexican Potatoes

Submitted by Janel Flynn

Recipe of my great aunt's that is awesomely delicious.

Boil 10–12 medium potatoes. Cool, peel, and cut into slices.

Combine:

¾ cup chopped onion
¾ cup green pepper, chopped
1 cup mayo
¾ cup milk
2 tsp. salt
1 tsp. pepper
1 cup American cheese, grated
¾ cup green olives and ripe black olives, mixed

Arrange in layers. Save ½ cup grated cheese to put on top. Bake at 375 degrees for 20–30 minutes.

Pot Roast with Dumplings

Submitted by Della Williamson

I got this recipe over forty years ago. I saw the recipe, and the dumplings caught my eye first. The kids were always asking for them. So I took a closer look at the recipe. Wasn't too sure about how well all the ingredients would work but gave it a try anyway. It was scrumptious and quickly became a family favorite. When cooked for company people usually ended up asking for the recipe. When I find an interesting recipe I follow it exactly the first time. After that, I experiment. The aroma from this pot roast fills the house with a delicious smell.

¼ cup butter
½ cup chopped onion
4 lb. chuck roast
1 bay leaf, crumbled
2 tbs. grated orange peel (zest)
1 tsp. salt
⅛ tsp. pepper
¼ tsp. allspice
10 oz. can beef consommé

Melt butter in skillet, then add chopped onions. When onions start to soften a bit, add the roast and sear. Then place into a Dutch oven and add the rest of the ingredients. Loosely cover. Simmer for 3½ to 4 hours, or until beginning to become fork tender. Add a can of water and bring to a boil. While it is coming to a boil mix your dumplings.

Dumplings:

2 cups Bisquick
⅔ cup milk

Mix till soft dough forms.

Drop by spoonfuls into boiling liquid in Dutch oven. Cook uncovered for 10 minutes, then cover and cook for another 10 minutes.

Alternative:

1 cup chopped onion (we really like onions, so I usually use a whole cup; it doesn't affect the taste)
4 lb. chuck roast (actually any would do; I've found it doesn't really matter. Even the toughest, cheapest cut becomes fork tender)

2 10-oz. cans beef consommé
2 tbs. grated orange peel (zest)
¼ tsp. allspice
2 bay leaves, crumbled (I used 2 torn in half)
1 tsp. salt
⅛ tsp. pepper

In a Dutch oven, place the chopped onion and then put the meat on that. Pour in the 2 cans of beef consommé.

Sprinkle the orange peel and allspice *on* the meat with some bleed over into the liquid. The bay leaves are placed in the liquid around the meat. Cover loosely and simmer. After about 3½hours, if it is getting fork tender, I add 2 cans of water. Salt and pepper to taste.

Bisquick Dumplings:

2 cups Bisquick
⅔ cups milk

Mix till soft dough forms.

Drop by spoonfuls into boiling liquid in Dutch oven. Cook uncovered for 10 minutes. Then cover and cook for another 10 minutes.

Serve, using the liquid in Dutch oven as a gravy for dumplings.

Corn Casserole

Submitted by Pamela Curran

2 tbs. margarine
2 tbs. flour
2 tbs. chopped onion
8 oz. carton sour cream
2 cans whole kernel corn
12 slices bacon

Sauté the first three ingredients and add the sour cream. Beat until cream melts. Drain the whole kernel corn and add to the sour cream mixture. Fry the 12 slices of bacon until crisp and crumble 6 into this mixture. Use the remaining bacon on top of the casserole. Bake at 350 degrees for 30 minutes.

Peanut Butter Brownie Cake

Submitted by Teri Fish

My grandma, Hazel Taylor, used to make this for my mom and aunt's birthdays and maybe one other time during the year. It brings back memories of my grandma and mom.

½ cup butter
1 cup sugar
2 eggs
1 tsp. vanilla
1 cup Hershey's Chocolate Syrup
1¼ cups unsifted flour
½ tsp. baking soda
1 cup peanut butter chips

Cream butter, sugar, eggs, and vanilla. Beat well. Add chocolate syrup and mix. Then add flour and baking soda and mix well. Mix in peanut butter chips. Pour into a greased 9 x 13 pan. Bake at 350 degrees for 30–35 minutes. Cool cake before frosting.

Frosting:

½ cup sugar
¼ cup canned milk

2 tbs. butter
1 cup peanut butter chips
1 tsp. vanilla

Combine sugar, canned milk, and butter into a small pan. Stir over medium heat until it comes to a full rolling boil. Remove from stove quickly and add peanut butter chips and stir until melted. Add vanilla and beat to a spreading consistency and frost cake.

Triple Layer Pistachio Pie

Submitted by Vivian Shane

This is a visually appealing pie with its graduated colors in the three layers, which are a nice contrast to the dark Oreo crust.

2 oz. Baker's semi-sweet chocolate, melted
¼ cup sweetened condensed milk
1 Oreo pie crust
¾ cup chopped toasted pistachios
2 pkgs. (3.4 oz. each) Jell-O pistachio flavor instant pudding
1¾ cup cold milk
1 tub (8 oz.) whipped topping, thawed

Mix the chocolate and condensed milk until blended; spread onto bottom of crust. Sprinkle with half the nuts. Refrigerate until ready to use.

Beat the pudding mixes and milk with a whisk for 2 minutes (pudding will be thick). Spread
1½ cups over the chocolate layer in the crust. Stir half of the whipped topping into the remaining pudding and spread over the pudding layer in the crust. Top with the

remaining whipped topping and sprinkle with the remainder of the nuts. Refrigerate 3 hours or until firm.

Books by Kathi Daley

Come for the murder, stay for the romance. Buy them on Amazon today.

Zoe Donovan Cozy Mystery:

Halloween Hijinks
The Trouble With Turkeys
Christmas Crazy
Cupid's Curse
Big Bunny Bump-off
Beach Blanket Barbie
Maui Madness
Derby Divas
Haunted Hamlet
Turkeys, Tuxes, and Tabbies
Christmas Cozy
Alaskan Alliance
Matrimony Meltdown
Soul Surrender
Heavenly Honeymoon
Hopscotch Homicide
Ghostly Graveyard
Santa Sleuth
Shamrock Shenanigans

Zimmerman Academy Shorts

Shorts
The New Normal – *January 2016*

Paradise Lake Cozy Mystery:

Pumpkins in Paradise
Snowmen in Paradise
Bikinis in Paradise
Christmas in Paradise
Puppies in Paradise
Halloween in Paradise

Whales and Tails Cozy Mystery:

Romeow and Juliet
The Mad Catter
Grimm's Furry Tail
Much Ado About Felines
Legend of Tabby Hollow
Cat of Christmas Past
A Tale of Two Tabbies – *February 2016*

Seacliff High Mystery:

The Secret
The Curse
The Relic
The Conspiracy
The Grudge

Road to Christmas Romance:

Road to Christmas Past

Kathi Daley lives with her husband, kids, grandkids, and Bernese mountain dogs in beautiful Lake Tahoe. When she isn't writing, she likes to read (preferably at the beach or by the fire), cook (preferably something with chocolate or cheese), and garden (planting and planning, not weeding). She also enjoys spending time on the water when she's not hiking, biking, or snowshoeing the miles of desolate trails surrounding her home.

Kathi uses the mountain setting in which she lives, along with the animals (wild and domestic) that share her home, as inspiration for her cozy mysteries.

Stay up-to-date with her newsletter, *The Daley Weekly*. There's a link to sign up on both her Facebook page and her website, or you can access the sign-in sheet at: http://eepurl.com/NRPDf

Visit Kathi:

Facebook at Kathi Daley Books, www.facebook.com/kathidaleybooks

Kathi Daley Teen – www.facebook.com/kathidaleyteen

Kathi Daley Books Group Page – https://www.facebook.com/groups/569578823146850/

Kathi Daley Books Birthday Club- get a book on your birthday - https://www.facebook.com/groups/1040638412628912/

Kathi Daley Recipe Exchange - https://www.facebook.com/groups/752806778126428/

Webpage - www.kathidaley.com

E-mail - kathidaley@kathidaley.com

Recipe Submission E-mail – kathidaleyrecipes@kathidaley.com

Goodreads: https://www.goodreads.com/author/show/7278377.Kathi_Daley

Twitter at Kathi Daley@kathidaley - https://twitter.com/kathidaley

Tumblr - http://kathidaleybooks.tumblr.com/

Amazon Author Page - http://www.amazon.com/Kathi-Daley/e/B00F3BOX4K/ref=sr_tc_2_0?qid=1418237358&sr=8-2-ent

Pinterest - http://www.pinterest.com/kathidaley/

CPSIA information can be obtained
at www.ICGtesting.com
Printed in the USA
BVHW040826190320
575431BV00007B/153